LOVE BEYOND BODY, SPACE, AND TIME

AN INDIGENOUS LGBT SCI-FI ANTHOLOGY

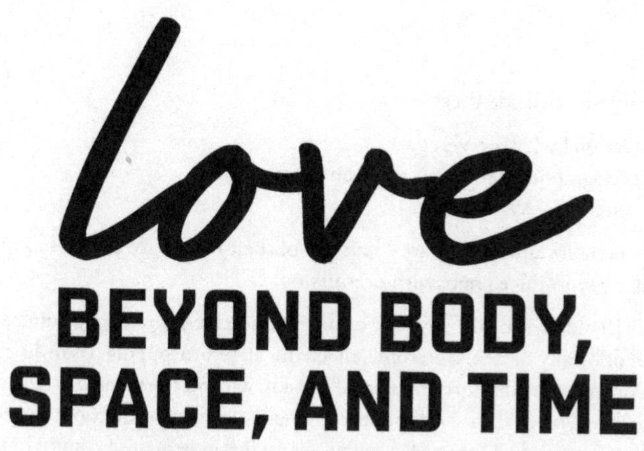

BEYOND BODY, SPACE, AND TIME

AN INDIGENOUS LGBT SCI-FI ANTHOLOGY

EDITED BY HOPE NICHOLSON
ADDITIONAL EDITS BY ERIN COSSAR & SAM BEIKO

Cover illustration by Jeffrey Veregge
Design & Typography by Relish New Brand Experience
Printed in Canada by Webcom

LIBRARY AND ARCHIVES CANADA CATALOGUING IN PUBLICATION

Love beyond body, space, and time / edited by Hope Nicholson.

Issued in print and electronic formats.

ISBN 978-0-9939970-7-5 (paperback).--ISBN 978-0-9939970-6-8 (pdf)

1. Science fiction, Canadian (English). 2. Fantasy fiction, Canadian (English). 3. Short stories, Canadian (English). 4. Short stories, American. 5. Native peoples in literature. 6. Indian gays in literature. 7. Two-spirit people in literature. 8. Sexual minorities in literature. 9. Gays in literature. I. Nicholson, Hope, 1986-, editor

PS8323.S3L68 2016 C813'.08760806 C2016-904904-3
C2016-904905-1

BEDSIDE PRESS
http://bedsidepress.com

•●•●•●•

CONTENTS

•●•●•●•

LETTER FROM THE EDITOR

by Hope Nicholson

I WAS RELUCTANT TO WRITE A FOREWORD for this collection, as these are not my stories to tell. But there are some questions that are asked of me often. Why do you think these stories are important to be told? Why have you pushed so hard to make *Love Beyond Body, Space, and Time* above any other book? And so, here is why I created this book.

When I first began my publishing company, Bedside Press, the aim of the projects I chose and curated were that they would share stories that needed to be told. This was idealistic, and in some ways foolish. Not all stories, despite their rarity and scarcity, should be told to everyone. Sometimes the act of sharing changes and simplifies the stories and the experiences they represent. There are reasons why many transgender people do not discuss aspects of their transition. There are reasons why many indigenous creators do not tell stories publicly to those outside their community. Stories, when they're told, have an enormous opportunity to connect people, to bind hearts and minds and stories, to make one feel like they're not alone. I strongly believe in this. And this must be balanced always, with people's privacy, sense of self, and sense of community, which must remain intact. Not all stories need to be shared, because the act of sharing makes them vulnerable to change and exploitation. It's my aim to be aware of this and sensitive to this in my projects.

I'm honoured that the creators in this anthology have chosen these stories to be shared. I selected the genres of speculative fiction, science-fiction, and fantasy for this collection as it is my belief that there is a tendency to restrict indigenous stories to one time, one place, and force culture to be something to be looked at from a distance. I hope that by having stories unburdened by time, place, or space, that it creates connection. And I just really love outer-space, time travel, and magic stories!

All of the creators in this anthology identify as indigenous. Most identify as queer, as bisexual, as lesbian, as transgender, as two-spirit. Some do not, but are supportive of their friends and family who are, and are eager to write stories of experiences outside of their own.

I chose these creators from a curated list of writers who I dearly wanted to work with, some were recommended to me from friends, and others came on board from an open call for submissions. Their experience range significantly, but each is a skilled storyteller.

These are stories that are told slowly and quickly, of the future and the now, the here and the there. These are stories of people falling in love with bodies and minds unexpectedly. These are people who are learning to love themselves. These are not my stories but they touch me, and they make me see the world outside as even more bright and beautiful than I did before I read them, and I know they will for you too.

•●•●•●•

BEYOND THE GRIM DUST OF WHAT *WAS* TO A RADIANT POSSIBILITY OF WHAT *COULD BE*: Two-Spirit Survivance Stories

by Grace L. Dillon

TWO-SPIRIT NATURES SWIM HARD among strong cultural currents, resisting both colonial gender binaries and sexual regimes imposed by the legacy of nineteenth-century white manifest destinies, as well as skepticism and rejection by some traditional Native communities. Two-Spirit stories are at their core survivance stories. *Biskaabiiyang*, Anishinaabemowin for "returning to ourselves," is a healing impulse and a manifesto for all peoples, whether Indigenous or just passing through, about discarding the dirty baggage imposed by the impacts of oppression, and alternatively refashioning ancestral traditions in order to flourish in the post-Native Apocalypse.

Little wonder that science fiction (SF) and the possibility of imagining present futures appeals to two-spirit writers, to Native writers, and, as this collection shows, to two-spirit Native writers. SF survivance stories are not about survival. SF survivance stories are about persistence, adaptation, and flourishing in the future, in sometimes subtle but always important contrast to mere survival, or the self-limiting experience of trauma and loss that often surrenders the imagination to creeds of isolation and victimhood, the apprehension of hopeless, helpless entitlement to an extirpated past. SF survivance stories project near and far futures where Indigenous peoples reclaim sovereignty and self-determination. Qwo-Li Driskill and others speak of "the decolonial potential of Native two-spirit/queer people healing from heteropatriarchal gender regimes."

Biskaabiiyang.

Strong voices share the survivance stories collected here, echoing precedents, a tradition worth remembering and recalling: Beth Brant's *A Gathering of Spirit: A Collection of Writing and Art by North American Indian Women* (1984); editor Will Roscoe's collaborative offering with the Gay American Indians (GAI) advocacy group, *Living the Spirit: A Gay American Indian Anthology* (1988); Lester B. Brown, *Two Spirit People: American Indian Lesbian Women and Gay Men* (1997); Will Roscoe, *Changing Ones: Third and Fourth Genders in Native North America* (2000); Qwo-Li Driskill's "Stolen from Our Bodies: First Nations Two-Spirits/Queers and the Journey to a Sovereign Erotic" (*Studies in American Indian Literatures*, 2004); editors Qwo-Li Driskill, Daniel Heath Justice, Deborah Miranda, and Lisa Tatonetti's *Sovereign Erotics: A Collection of Two-Spirit Literature* (2011). Contributions to two-spirit understanding have emerged more recently in notable research efforts, including the 2010 special edition of *A Journal of Lesbian and Gay Studies on Sexuality, Nationality, Indigeneity* edited by Daniel Heath Justice, Mark Rifkin, and Bethany Schneider; Qwo-Li Driskill, Chris Finley, Brian Joseph Gilley and Scott Lauria Morgensen, *Queer Indigenous Studies: Critical Interventions in Theory, Politics, and Literature* (2011); Scott Lauria Morgensen, *Spaces Between Us: Queer Settler Colonialism and Indigenous Decolonization* (2011); Mark Rifkin, *When Did Indians Become Straight?: Kinship, the History of Sexuality, and Native Sovereignty* (2011); and Rifkin's more recent *Erotics of Sovereignty: Queer Native Writing in the Era of Self-Determination* (2012).

Love Beyond Body, Space, and Time returns us to ourselves as agents of our own destinies, however uncertain, scary, and dangerous our acquisitions are bound to become. Here you will meet heroes who search inwardly and vigorously on futurescapes where two-spirit and transgender identities remain marginalized but hopeful. The notion of survivance broadens to foreground gender and sexuality in the context of ameliorated *Indian* futures, reminding us that social justice and equality for all GLBTQ2 communities remains a preeminent human rights issue of our time.

Grace L. Dillon
Portland State University

•●•●•●•

RETURNING TO OURSELVES: Two Spirit Futures and the Now

by Niigaan Sinclair

> Two-spirit people—identified by many different tribally-specific names and community positions—have been living, loving, and creating art since time immemorial. (1)—*Qwo-Li Driskill, Daniel Heath Justice, Deborah Miranda, and Lisa Tatonetti*

ON JANUARY 2, 1801, fur trader Alexander Henry met an Anishinaabe named Ozawwendib ("Yellow Head") in his travels across the Great Lakes. A child of the great Anishinaabe chief Wiishkobak ("Sweet"), Ozawwendib perplexed Henry. As he described in his journal:

> This person is a curious compound of man and woman. He is a man both as to his members and his courage, but pretends to be womanish, and dresses as such. His walk and mode of sitting, his manners, occupations, and language are those of a woman. His father, who is a great chief amongst the Saulteurs, cannot persuade him to act like a man. (163)

Henry also remarks that Ozawwendib is an incredible hunter and courageous warrior but "troublesome when drunk" (163).

Years later, John Tanner, a settler adopted into the Anishinaabeg, met Ozawwendib on the shores of the Red River near Pembina. Referring to Ozawwendib as "one of those who make themselves women, and are called women by the Indians," Tanner narrates an odd tale of their encounter:

> This creature, called Ozaw-wend-dib, (the yellow head,) was now near fifty years old, and had lived with many husbands. I do not know whether she had seen me, or only heard of me, but she soon let me know she had come a long distance to see me, and with the hope of living with me. She often offered herself to me, but not being discouraged with one refusal, she repeated her disgusting advances until I was almost driven from the lodge. (89-90)

Encouraged by his adopted Anishinaabe mother to pursue the relationship, Tanner condemns Ozawwendib's "offers" until she asks him to kill a moose she sees. After failing to kill the moose, Ozawwendib then ironically denies Tanner, marrying another man. Tanner's narcissistic description of Ozawwendib's advances, his copious narrative detail, and equation of his failure to provide alongside Ozawwendib's rejection suggest that Tanner doth protest too much.

These would not be the only historical accounts of Ozawwendib. Ethnologist Henry Schoolcraft, for example, would fondly remark that Ozaawindib was very courageous and guided him (20). Ozawwendib's abilities would also lead to her sharing her name with two water bodies: Ozaawindibe-zaaga'igan (later renamed Lake Plantagenet) and Ozaawindibe-ziibi (later renamed Schoolcraft River). Clearly, many respected Ozawwendib and defined her by her many accomplishments and abilities.

For Henry and Tanner, however, Ozawwendib's biology and sexuality is all they are interested in. Like much of where homophobia comes from, science and social behaviour are constructed at oppositions and deemed irreconcilable and "disgusting." Add in that Ozawwendib is an "Indian" and what emerges is a plethora of nineteenth-century misrepresentations and judgements. Their narratives suggest that Ozawwendib represented an ideological, moral, and cultural abnormality; a person to be wondered at, judged, and in need of civilization. Ozawwendib was a primitive, alien life form; "discovered," singularly-defined, and deficient.

Activist and theorist David Thorstad remarks that "Ozawwendib was not a transvestite but a male who lived, dressed, walked and talked like a female and who had sex with 'normal' males" ("On 'Sweet,' 'Yellow Head,' and 'Two-Spirit'"). Perhaps. Whether Ozawwendib is definable by what we may now call transsexual or homosexual (or whatever else!) is to overlook two important points, though. The first is that in the time and place Ozawwendib lived, this "curious compound of man and woman" did not "fit" into Western and European sexual and gender norms—and perhaps even Anishinaabeg, too (see: Henry's comments about Wiishkobak attempting to "persuade [him] to act like a man"). For most around her, Ozawwendib's sexual, physical, and cultural identity is undefinable. The second is that Ozawwendib appeared to live without shame, apology, and fear. In fact, Ozawwendib thrived. She clearly cared for and worked in the interests of community, living with a tremendous amount of agency over her body, identity, and definition.

Ozawwendib was not an abnormality. Indigenous communities have always had what we now refer to as lesbian, gay, bisexual, transgender/transsexual, queer, or what Anishinaabe today refer as *niizh-manidoowag*—two-spirit. Going by many names (most often within tribal languages), Indigenous LGBTQ and two-spirit peoples formed—and continue to form—one of the most important part of our cultures, communities, and traditions today.

Defining an Indigenous LGBTQ and two-spirit tradition is as complicated as describing Indigenous peoples themselves. As Driskill, Justice, Miranda, and Tatonetti state: "Queer Native people are far from a monolithic group. We have numerous identities, artistic stances, and political agendas. We come from diverse nations, land bases, and traditions." Even naming this tradition is complex. While many terms are utilized—including problematic and inappropriate terms like "berdache"—two-spirit is the one perhaps most often used today. Two-spirit is a term founded at the third Native American/First Nations Gay and Lesbian Conference in Winnipeg in 1990. It was intended to gesture to Indigenous notions of gender outside of Western male and female binaries while at the same time suggesting that certain sexual, social, and relational identities exist in Indigenous communities beyond anthropocentric formations. Some do not like the term, however, and use LGBTQ or definitions in their own ancestral languages.

Like Ozawwendib, Indigenous LGBTQ and two-spirit peoples are undefinable by biology and sexual orientation—although these may make up a part of their identities. Indigenous LGBTQ and two-spirit peoples performed essential and critical roles in all aspects of Indigenous life. Indigenous communities incorporated, accepted, and honoured LGBTQ and two-spirit lives in ceremonies, families, governments, and the everyday. As Northern Paiute writer Randy Burns describes: "We lived openly in our tribes. Our families and communities recognized us and encouraged us to develop our skills. In turn, we made special contributions to our communities" (1). For millennia, Indigenous sexuality, gender definitions, and social formations existed in a universal paradigm of multiplicity and complexity, tied to place, time, and the world around communities, incorporating everything in the corporeal and incorporeal universes surrounding them. Generally, most Indigenous communities sought healthy, balanced, and reciprocal relationships based on processes of gift-giving, sharing, and interdependency with those around them. No community was perfect, of course, but those who incorporated the widest sense of relationship-making often thrived and continued in the strongest path.

Indigenous LGBTQ and two-spirit peoples gifted their communities some of the greatest expressions of relationship making, carrying knowledge and experience on how to form ties using the body, spirit, and other parts of life. Fuelled often by a love for land, community, and forces in the universe, sex was only a form of exchange for Indigenous LGBTQ and two-spirit peoples—and definitely not the only one. In the songs, words, and stories of Indigenous LGBTQ and two-spirit community members, notions of responsibility, generosity, and intellectual production forming the foundation of Indigenous communities could be found. To do this, Indigenous LGBTQ and two-spirit artists not only became knowledge-makers in their community's cultural, political, and ideological frameworks, but in scientific discourses. They illustrated that, to form relationships with the world, one must understand all of it, using all ways. Lastly—and really not needing to be said—Indigenous LGBTQ and two-spirit traditions continue today.

At the same time, and again like Ozawwendib, Indigenous LGBTQ and two-spirit peoples have experienced what Burns calls "double oppression—both racism and homophobia" (2) over time. Draconian influences of a Victorian, normalizing, Euro-centric and Western sense of sexuality and identity have sought to oppress, punish, and erase Indigenous LGBTQ and two-spirit traditions from the landscape of North America. As the writers of The Just Society Report: *Grossly Indecent: Confronting the Legacy of State Sponsored Discrimination Against Canada's LGBTQ2SI Communities* write:

> ...what we would now classify as homophobia, biphobia, and transphobia were clearly introduced by European settlers, founded in and encouraged by the state-sanctioned Christian religion and enforced through the criminal laws of the state.
>
> The introduction and flourishing of what we now characterize as homophobia, biphobia, and transphobia can be directly related to the systematic dismantling of Aboriginal culture by European colonizers and Canada that has been appropriately characterized as "cultural genocide."
>
> The notion that such gender and sexual non-conforming behaviour was sinful, criminal, or symptomatic of disease was entirely unknown among Aboriginal Peoples prior to Contact. Prior to Contact, the region of North America now known as Canada was relatively free of these destructive negative social attitudes. (15)

I would add that science has been the predominant foundation for arguments supporting colonial hatred and fear of Indigenous LGBTQ and two-spirit traditions. Arguments based in biased and Darwinian understandings of science, constructing what is "normal," "civilization," and "order" formed the basis for Christian ideas of "natural law" and legal principles that legislated and justified hate. These systems perpetuated violence against Indigenous peoples and created cycles that undermined community principles, divided families and clans, and constituted not only "cultural genocide" but actual, physical genocide.

For over three centuries Indigenous LGBTQ and two-spirit communities have been enduring waves of hate embodied in laws, practices, and discourses across North America. While at times difficult to discern from the violence all Indigenous communities endure, Indigenous LGBTQ and two-spirit communities have experienced specific social and political ostracization, violence, and erasure. Much of this has been done through writing. From laws to media to representations in novels and poems, Indigenous LGBTQ and two-spirit identities have been manipulated, misrepresented, and mutated into written figments of settler desire and fear. Unfortunately, many Indigenous communities have adopted these ideologies and perpetuate lateral violence on their relatives, too, isolating the very traditions that formed the basis for our cultural and intellectual livelihoods.

Still, Indigenous two-spirit identities endure and thrive. In fact, Indigenous two-spirit community members continue to gift us one of the longest and most extensive stories of revolution and agency in North American history. Indigenous two-spirit artists have been using love to overcome hate across time and space—and even beyond it. It is not enough to call this work resistance; it is resilience. Indigenous LGBTQ and two-spirit peoples will be with us for as long as Indigenous communities continue.

Love Beyond Body, Space, and Time: An Indigenous LGBT Sci-Fi Anthology is a recognition of Indigenous LGBTQ and two-spirit traditions. These stories display a commitment, responsibility, and resilience—love—that has never left Indigenous life. They honour the history in what they emerge but, radically, none of these stories are solely about history. These narratives are about the future, time-travel, and other worlds. They are visions and re-visions of a complete and full Indigenous tomorrow.

Most importantly, these stories use science—one of the most powerful discourses that have been used to "civilize" Indigenous communities—and fiction—the other tool that has been used to misrepresent and mutate our lives—and re-makes them. They gift us ways of seeing reality beyond that which we have inherited and see science and fiction for what it always should have given us: dreams, hope, and possibilities beyond what we think we see.

If there is one central theme in this collection (among many) it is the revolutionary power of love to form, recreate, and empower relationships. Some of the stories are about sex but much more are not, illustrating the gifts Indigenous LGBTQ and two-spirit peoples use to enact a spectrum of ties in the interests of Indigenous life-making across corporeal and incorporeal realities. These stories are about bodies, words, and actions to evoke growth, change, and life. A love more than Hollywood nonsense but the hard work that commitment, responsibility, and growth takes when you love another.

In the following stories you will read how love is found when travelling to other worlds, such as in "Né łe!" by Darcie Little Badger, a narrative about a romance during a migration to Mars. This is also uncovered in David Robertson's "Perfectly You," a story of how love can defeat time—no matter the distance. There are stories of dynamic Indigenous familial relations such as in Cherie Dimaline's "Legends are Made, Not Born" or the growth and multiplicity of Indigenous identity via science and tradition in Gwen Benaway's "Transitions." Mari Kurisato's "Imposter Syndrome" is an illustration of how dancing, running, and movement can overcome all forces of stasis and violence. Cleo Keahna's incredible piece "Parallax," is a story-poem that not only reminds of the power of gender multiplicity but the ability of Indigenous traditions to change, grow, and expand into the future.

In this collection are some of the most vibrant love stories you will ever read as well, illustrating how a truthful and committed love can literally change the world in both Richard Van Camp's "Aliens" and Nathan Adler's "Valediction at the Star View Hotel." Daniel Heath Justice's "The Boys Who Became Hummingbirds: A Fabulous Fable" is a traditional story very much about the future; literally bending the power of beauty to overcome despair and blend past, present, and future into one. These stories will make you feel warm, inspired, and driven to create some of the passages that pass before your eyes in your own relationships and journey in life.

Recognizing Indigenous LGBTQ and two-spirit traditions is one of our most important tasks we have today as Indigenous and non-Indigenous peoples. *Love Beyond Body, Space, and Time* does this and I applaud Hope

Nicholson and her writers for helping us re-learn traditions that not only expand our relationships with the world, but equip us to deal with issues such as climate change, war, and peace. All of the Indigenous LGBTQ and two-spirit narratives in this collection gift us with unique opportunities to see what has always been there and how we can be more.

So let's read and enjoy, and let love guide us as we understand, work, and change.

Beyond body, space, and time.

Miigwech.

WORKS CITED

Burns, Randy. Preface. Living the Spirit: A Gay American Indian Anthology. Ed. Will Roscoe. New York: St. Martin's P, 1988. 1-5.

Driskill, Qwo-Li, Daniel Heath Justice, Deborah Miranda, and Lisa Tatonetti. Introduction.

Sovereign Erotics: A Collection of Two-Spirit Literature. Tucson: U of Arizona P, 2011. 1-20.

Egale Human Rights Trust. *The Just Society Report Grossly Indecent: Confronting the Legacy of State Sponsored Discrimination Against Canada's LGBTQ2SI Communities*. 2016. <http://egale.ca/wp-content/uploads/2016/06/FINAL_REPORT_EGALE.pdf>.

Gough, B., ed. *The Journal of Alexander Henry the Younger, 1799-1814*. Vol. 1. Toronto: Champlain Society, 1988.

Schoolcraft, Henry Rowe. *Narrative of an Expedition Through the Upper Mississippi to Itasca Lake: The Actual Source of This River.* New York: Harper & Brothers. 1834.

Tanner, John. *The Falcon: A Narrative of the Captivity and Adventures of John Tanner.* London: Penguin, 2003.

•●•●•●•

ALIENS

by Richard Van Camp (for Carla Ulrich)

I WANNA TELL YOU A BEAUTIFUL STORY. And I've been waiting for somebody very special to tell it to. I guess it's no secret now: the aliens or "Sky People" are here. We can see a ship way up high: its outline. No lights. It's like a big, dark stone in the sky and most people just watch TV or Facebook now, waiting for something to happen. Some people call them 'Obelisks.' Apparently, there's one huge ship miles high over every continent and the oceans are boiling, gently, but no fish are dying. Just simmering, and scientists are saying that the oceans and rivers are being cleansed. It's like the "Star People"—that's what our Elders call them—are helping us.

Church bells all over the world chime every hour on the hour but I'm not sure why. One of the young men here one night got drunk and took his dad's rifle and shot at the ship. When he woke up he didn't have hair. It was all there: right on his pillow. He's not hurt; he's just...embarrassed.

So some of us—like me—I still go to work. The Sky People are here but the bills don't stop. Plus you gotta get out of the house, right? You gotta check the mail and get groceries, hey?

I'm just gonna start. So as we get on in years, many of us have left Fort Smith. We've gone off to college, or university, or trade schools. Many of us have found relationships, lost relationships, re-found love, right? People have raised their children—some people I went to school with are grandparents now.

And I'm so proud of them. Nothing beats a Christmas concert at JBT Elementary on December 17th every year, right? 'Cause you look around onstage and you see the kids; you feel the pride in the room, that these are our families. We've raised them together. The people we went to school with, those are the teachers of my children right now, and we're all doing great. Everyone's healthy as far as I know...and I'm so grateful for that.

But there's one man who never really left town, and—I'm gonna call him Jimmy for the sake of this story. So Jimmy's family owns the hardware store—and he's always been quiet. He's always been gentle.

My grandfather once cured a relation of Jimmy's. My grandfather was a holy man. His name was *Edzazii*—No English—a very traditional Tłı̨chǫ Dene man. And they say my grandfather pulled a hummingbird of fire out of a little boy's mouth, from under his tongue. And he showed that little boy this little bird that had been living in his mouth. And he explained this was the reason that little boy couldn't speak like other people, and this is why his voice kept locking. And hundreds of people saw this little hummingbird that my grandfather pulled out of this little boy's mouth, and my ehtse let that little bird go over Marion Lake. They saw my ehtse's power. And when that bird of fire left, it flew like a 30/30 shot, and it exploded into sound and light. And my grandfather walked all the way back to that little boy, and he said, "Now speak." That little boy started to speak—and they said his knees were just shaking. And that little boy never stuttered again. That's Jimmy's dad. And they say every time he prays, he thanks my grandfather for releasing that little bird from his mouth.

So I guess you can say me and Jimmy are related in the medicine way.

Jimmy's always been in the background of our community. He's always been quiet. He's always been cruising around by himself. He's always standing, leaning against the back wall at the Christmas concert. Never goes up to dance at any of the gatherings. Never comes into the drum dance, now that the tea dance is back and the drum dance is back. Never participates in hand games. He will go for a burger, but he'll be last in line at Aboriginal Day or Canada Day. He'll wait around for, you know, the second run at the fish fry. He's never been one to go to the front. And I've always quietly wondered about him. I always wondered, like, *why didn't you leave?* Like, weren't you ever curious about the city? Weren't you ever curious about GM Place, or a hockey game...or Def Leppard coming to the city? Or didn't you ever wanna go and hang out at West Edmonton Mall, or go for a burger at Earl's or Bourbon Street? Like, why? When did you decide to live a quiet, gentle life?

'Cause the worry, from my point of view, is that his is a forgettable life. Because, who knew you? Who did you ever love? Who did you ever—who did you ever give yourself to? I always worried about that with him. I always wondered about that.

Well, little while ago, my niece told me that one time she was in the hardware store looking for lights. 'Member, there was that big rebate: if you switch your house to LED lights, you get, you know, free LED lights, and all that. Some government thing.

And, so my niece is in there one day, and Jimmy walked up to her and he said, "Uh, hi," he said. (We'll call her Shandra.) "Hi, Shandra," he says. "Can I help you?" and she says, "Oh, I'm looking for these LED lights—the government's giving a rebate?" And he says, "Oh yeah. They sold out really quick but we have more in the storage room." And she says, "Oh." He says, "I'll go...I'll go get 'em for you." She says, "Oh, thanks."

So he come back after a while and he said, "Well, I was wondering what you're doing tonight." And she said, "Oh, uh, I don't know—I'm just taking it easy, I guess." And he said, "Well I was wondering if I could take you out for supper." And she said, "Oh! Why?" And he said, "Well, I'd like to just—take you out for supper and get to talk with you." And she said, "Oh, like a date!" And he got really shy and he goes, "Well, if you wanna call it that." And so she said, "Oh, well, wow, yeah, what a surprise—okay, sure!" And he goes, "Well, do you want me to pick you up in my truck?" And she said, "Oh, no, I'll just walk there." And he says, "Oh, I'd love to pick you up in my truck." And she says, "Oh, no. It's okay, Jimmy, I'll—I'll just walk there." 'Cause she didn't want the town to see them driving around, right? 'Cause this is serious business, right? My niece knows her way.

Well, in a small town, this is very serious. Also, which part of the restaurant do you take your date? Do you go on the café side...or do you go to the *fancy* side?

So he said, "Uh, okay, ah, so, tonight, six o'clock?" And she said, "Okay, well, I'll meet you there!" And he goes, "Well, you know, do you want reservations under my name or yours?" And she said, "Oh! Well, uh, maybe yours, Jimmy," and he said, "Okay," and he goes, "So six o'clock: reservations under my name?" And he said, "I want you to know it's on me. Anything that you want...This is really special to me and I want it to be special for you." And she said, "Are you serious? Like you're talkin' steak and lobster?" And he goes, "Whatever you want." And she said, "Oh, I was just kidding. I would never order steak and lobster." And he goes, "Well, we should. We should order steak and lobster!" She says, "Wow, Jimmy, this is...this is really—sweet! Okay." "Okay, well, I'll see you there," he smiles. "Maybe after we could go to the Landslide and watch the Star People. At around ten o'clock there's a hum to the ship you can feel in the earth. Like, if you take off your shoes." And she says, "Oh, well now: we'll see. I should go." So was really flustered. And he goes, "Well, don't you want your lights?" And she said, "Waaah, I just, I need to think about this." And he goes, "Well, what's to think about?" And she said, "It's just that, um—a lot of people who ask me out on dates, it's not because they want me—it's because they want my friend Roberta."

And he said, "Roberta?" He says, "I don't...know Roberta. I don't really wanna know her. You know, I'm happy she's your best friend, but," he said, "I'm interested in you." And she said, "Well, you have to excuse me. I'm really surprised, 'cause you never really talked to me before." And he says, "Well, we say hi." And she goes, "Well, yeah, but barely" And she goes, "I don't want to make you feel bad or anything. It's just, I'm so surpr—I'm honoured, I'm excited, I'm nervous. It's been years since anybody's asked me out." And he said, "Well, I'm really surprised to hear that." And she goes, "Well, it's true." And he goes, "I promise you, it's—I'm not after Roberta," he says, "I'm after you." And she's like, "Well, you know, Jimmy, if we go for a date, this changes everything. You realize that." And he goes, "Well... that's what I'm counting on."

"Well, son of a gun," she said. "Okay, well, I'm gonna go...I'm gonna go for a walk. I need to think about this. I want to get a little dressed up for tonight." And he goes, "Well, I'll get dressed up, too." And she says, "Okaaaay. So see you tonight at six." And he goes, "Well, what are we gonna do about these lights?" And she says, "Well, let's see how this date goes."

And he says, "Oh! Okay—well, they'll be waitin' here for you." And she says, "Well, never mind that. I gotta go home and get ready." Right, so, what she did was she went home, and she started calling around to all of us aunties, and she asked us, "What do we really know about Jimmy? Like, why is he alone? Why's he been alone?" Nobody could come up with anything. And she said, "Listen, don't tell anybody, but I'm going on a date." And we're like "*Gasp!* Oh my God! As soon as it's over you have to call!" Right? "Let us know what he's like—whether it's tomorrow morning, or at 7:30 tonight when you come home." This was better than *Young and the Restless*! She said, "Okay, okay, but don't tell anybody!" And we said, "To our graves. To our graves!" Top secret but we were on speakerphone crossing our fingers, hey? Yep. So, she got a little gussied up, and she went to the Pelican, and, sure enough, Jimmy was there. And he was dressed up.

She'd never seen him like this before. He shaved, you know, nice little black turtleneck, no clunky gold chain or anything, just dressed quite nicely. He's a new man. And they ordered—he insisted that they order the steak and lobster. And they had the Ginger Ale mixed with cranberry juice, "Indian champagne," they call it. Yep. And they had a really beautiful supper.

And she said, "Well, now that I've got you all to myself, like, I really wanna ask you something." And he said, "Anything you want." So she said, "Like, you've always lived—like, a gentle, quiet life. Didn't you ever want to leave?" And he said, "Not really." And so she says, "Well, like, aren't you curious about the city?" And he says, "No." And she says, "Well, do you ever go down to Edmonton?" And he goes, "Oh, I go down once or twice a year, and I get, you know, some new clothes, and a haircut, and, you know,

I—I go to a concert, or a hockey game." And she goes, "Well, do you ever travel with anyone?" And he said, "No, I just go by myself." She goes, "Like, where do you stay?" And he's like, "Oh, I just stay at a hotel. And she asks, "Have you always been a loner?" And he goes, "Well, kind of."

And so she says, "I'm just so curious about you, 'cause," she says, "I've, you know, I've gone out with people. I've broken up with people. I've never had children—I would like to have children one day. Would you like to have children?" And he says, "Oh! I'd—I'd love to have children, sure, with the right person." And so she says, "I'm just, I'm sitting here with you, and I realize, I've known you my whole life, but I don't really know you." And he says, "Well, I'm hoping that will change tonight. 'Cause you can ask me anything."

And so, they started to talk, and they started to visit, and they started to go back through elementary, and PWK memories...and you know, all this other good stuff, all the experiences they shared. But she got to hear it and see it from his eyes. And he actually had a really rough time growing up. He was bullied. He wasn't very athletic. You know, Smith is a hockey town, it's a baseball town. And he never really wanted to party. He was never really into smoking, or drinking, or toking, or anything like that. He likes his country, right? Like, George Jones, and Hank, and, you know, the oldies and the goldies. And so, they had the most beautiful meal, and he insisted they get warm apple pie and ice cream, and coffee. And they were just—in this island, together. And she was thinking, "This, this could be it. This could be the one! And he was here all along! How could I have missed Jimmy? You know, at the hardware store."

So, finally, now he says, "Well, can I—give you a ride in my truck?" And she says, "Oh, sure! Where do you wanna go?" And he goes, "Well, you wanna go for a cruise to the Landslide, or you want me to drop you off, or you wanna come back to my house?" And she says, "Well, where do you, where do you live?" And he said, "Oh, I live on—I live above the, you know, the, uh, hardware store." And she goes, "You live on top of there?" And he says, "Oh, it's beautiful! I've got a wide open concept, and I've got a big screen TV, and I have the—I can see the church, and I can see the northern lights, and I can look over and see the banks of the Slave River.

I can't see the Sky People from my window but it's pretty sweet." And she said, "Are you serious? I had no idea that there was a home above there." And he goes, "Oh, it makes sense. People try and break in all the time now." She says, "I didn't know that." And he says, "Oh, yeah. Well, Fort Smith has really changed over the years. So anytime I hear somebody messing around I go runnin' down there. I got a bullhorn, and usually scare people away. Most of the—most of the town here, they're pretty gentle, but, you know, every once in awhile, you get people who are drinking, and they're trying to get into the cash register, and, you know, drugs are really big in our town now." And she said, "Oh, I had no idea!"

And he says, "So, your house, go for a cruise, or my house?" And she said, "Well, I gotta see your house. I wanna see how you decorate." And he says, "Okay." So they drive to his house and then they get out—and he says, "Well, let me go up and I'll turn on all the lights for you and I'll call you." "Okay." And so she waited at the bottom of the stairs around the back. And she's like, "Son of a gun, I had no idea that he lived on top of this hardware store." And she's like, "Well, we'll find out, is he a hoarder? Is he cheap? Is it stinky?"

So he says, "Okay, come up!" And so she went upstairs, and he'd lit candles all the way up the stairs. I guess he'd already had them prepared and he had one of those little barbecue lighters. And there were hundreds of Christmas lights set up. And she said it was a beautiful home. It was actually very beautiful. And it was wide open, like you could see the futon; you could see his kitchen: it was all clean, and there's pictures of our leaders, you know, taken through the years that he'd had framed. He really loved our little town. He was like a little, quiet historian. And they could hear the rapids even better. And so she said, "Hey, I really love your place" and he says, "Oh thanks, I did it all myself, and I painted it, and I did all the woodwork...and I re-did all the tiles." She's like, "My God. You are one heck of a man!" And he said, "Well thank you! That means a lot coming from you."

And so she says, "I'm just so pleasantly surprised," and he says, "Well, would you...do you wanna have more coffee, or do you wanna have, like, some water? I don't really drink juice or anything." And she says, "Well, maybe just a glass of water," and he says, "Why don't you go have a shower?" And she says, "Have a shower?"

And he goes "Yeah, why don't you go have a shower?" And she says, "Well, why don't *you* go have a shower, Jimmy?" And he goes, "Oh, I already had a shower right before our feast."

And she says, "Okay, so you realize if I have a shower in your bathroom that, we're not goin' back from that?"

And he goes, "That's what I'm counting on."

And she said, "Did you really just tell me to go have a shower?"

And he grins, "Yeah." He says, "I love my women all showered up and fresh." She says, "*My women* no less! How many women have you had?" And he says, "Oh not too many, but I know what I like...and I like you." She thinks about this. It's been so long since she's been with anyone and every day could be our last with what's happening now in the world. "Okay," she says. "I'm gonna go have a shower, 'cause I want to see how this is gonna go—and when I come out, I'm gonna be wearing a towel...and what are you going to be wearing?" And he says, "You'll find out," and he winks, no less! So she goes and has a shower and she's like, "Son of a gun. I can't believe that I'm having a shower on top of the hardware store in Fort Smith. I'm about to come out and we're gonna see what's gonna happen." And she thought, "Wait a minute! What if Jimmy's a pervert and he's got cameras all set up?" And she goes, "Ah forget it. Who cares, right? It's just me. There's aliens in the frickin' sky so who cares if there's a recording of me towelling off." So she has a shower. She gets all gussied up, and she comes around the corner and he was naked on the bed.

So here's what happened next: they didn't actually go through second or third base. That's what we're being told, anyway. They kissed; they held each other; they spooned, but she came home about maybe two in the morning (that's what time *she says* she came, anyways). She called us early the next morning to prove she woke up in her own bed, and she said, "I need your advice." And we put her on speakerphone: "Oh my God, what?" And she said, "Jimmy's different." We looked at each other with bug eyes and our perms from '82 almost popped back. "What do you mean? Was he rough? Was he mean to you?"

And she said, "No, not at all." And we said, "Well, what? Tell us. Like, should we call the cops? Do you want us to get Flinch to go over there and beat him up?" And she said "No, he's—he's *beautiful*." And we said, "Well, like, what do you mean?" We're trappers' daughters so we're curious about everything, hey? And so she said "I—I can't actually, there are no words, for what he is, but he's so beautiful." And one of my sisters said, "Oh, sweetie. Is he really big? You know what, honey...I had one of those once, and you just, you just breathe. You just pick a point on the wall and you just focus and you just *breathe*. You just...you just breathe and it's like reverse Lamaze, and you just, you gotta breathe and push through it. Your body will accommodate."

Shandra said, "I'm gonna hang up now because this is not what I was going for."

There's giggles and squeals on the line as we start texting each other going, "Stagaatz!" and "Mah!" but the Aunty message was the same: "Okay, call us back tomorrow when you've had a good sleep," we said. So she called her best friend Roberta, I guess. And she said, "I need your advice. I—I really need your help." And Roberta says, "What happened? What what what?" And she said, "Jimmy is...he's really different. I've never been in this situation before." And Roberta said, "Oh my god. Your aunties just called and said Jimmy's hung like a horse? Because...you know, if he is, he doesn't need a little thing like you. He needs a woman like me, okay? I have birthed *twins*...okay? I can take care of that man. And if you're telling me what I think you're telling me—not that it's everything, but it doesn't hurt. Well, sometimes it kinda does...but the key here—"

And so, Shandra said she's kept it a secret, all this time, because she's always fought—this love that's waiting because of what he is, and who he is, and how he is. And she's never told us exactly who or what Jimmy is. But in my mind he's what the Crees say: Aayahkwew: neither man or woman but both. I really do. And I had a dream after she told me that. I had a dream of them lying together in bed, and they were holding each other.

And he asked her the most interesting question. He asked, "Do you ever have guests stay at your house?" And she said, "Oh yeah, all the time—I got cousins, and, you know, my relations. They pass through all the time." And he said, "Do you ever not do the bedding, right away?" And she said, "You mean the laundry?" And he goes, "Yeah. Do you ever not do it for a couple days?" And she said, "No, I do it as soon as they're gone. In fact, most of our guests are trained. They'll bring their wet towels and their bedding to the laundry room and throw it in the wash."

And he said, "Next time you have someone stay at your house, don't do the bedding." And she said, "Why?" He said, "My grandfather was a shaman. And when you went to go see him, when you were fighting cancer, or a broken heart, leukemia, T.B....he would ask you for your favourite piece of clothing. For men it would be a cap, gauntlets, maybe a favourite shirt. For women it might be a scarf, a shirt, a sweater, a jacket that they've had for years. And he used to put it in his pillowcase and he used to dream. And they said he could see your life, he could dream your life. And he would tell you the next day who was making you sick, what was making you sick, or how you were keeping yourself sick. That's why so many of us, we cut our nails, and we burn our nail clippings or we keep our hair, we burn our hair, or every time we blow our nose, we burn the Kleenex. Because all it takes is for somebody to get one of those pieces of you, and they have your spirit. They have you. They have a grip on you."

And he said, "I did leave Fort Smith once for a summer, and I helped out my auntie and uncle in High Level. And they had a little motel. And I would, you know, I had the run of the place, because most guests wouldn't get in until late. And I would always nap in the beds that people had slept in. And I would always see their life." And he said, "Try it sometime. Wait 'til you see what kind of dreams you can have. People leave their dreams behind."

I had that dream after she told me. And I think that he is a shaman. I think he's a modern-day shaman living in Fort Smith, and our community. And even though they're not an official couple, she's never been with anyone else.

She's never wanted to be with anyone else, but she's fighting—marriage, and she's fighting children for now...because I think she's trying to decide if she's willing to live with a shaman and someone who's both. And what does that mean in our communities right now? It's easy to be persecuted if you're two-spirited, or gay, or transgender, or both, or perhaps something we've never heard of before—even under these new skies.

So that's the story that's on my mind these days, is about what kind of love they have. And I want laughter for them; I want children for them, if that's what they want. I want to see them standing together, with me and my sisters, on December 17th at JBT Elementary, rooting for their kids and crying at the same time—with the rest of us, even with the Star People above hopefully helping us all.

Mahsi cho.

•●•●•●•

LEGENDS ARE MADE, NOT BORN

by Cherie Dimaline

MY MOM WAS A CATHOLIC HALFBREED who named me after a pack of smokes, Semaa-tobacco. She died in a fiery blaze of glory winning a snowmobile race. My father, also a Catholic halfbreed, had no say in what I was to be named and wasn't around to explain her death. He's less important here, though he did remain a steady if infrequent fixture in my later life until he died, less adventurously, at eighty-four, in an old age home.

The night of the race I was at my grandma's house. She was supposed to be watching me but I always felt it was more of a mutual watching. At six, she decided it was high-time I started to pull my own weight in euchre; after all, our family had a sharking reputation to uphold. There was even a cursing cut of the cards one could do when shuffling that was named after us.

We were at the kitchen table, a cloud of dense cigarette smoke hanging overhead like an ethereal chandelier. I was just slapping down the Jack of Spades over Grandma's ace, she was just beginning the opening syllable of her best French swear word, when my uncle Travis barged in the front door. His eyes were as wild as his hair, a spiky curled mullet that that was now fringed down across his forehead with melting snow. He looked like a bush man, a trapper half-mad with lonely fear. Something in his eyes made my tummy crunch up with the hot pinch of sudden urine.

One look to the door, to her youngest son, and Grandma finished her swear. "Tabernacle! What's wrong with you?"

He slid those eyes over to me, sitting there in my mustard-coloured Winnie the Pooh pajamas with the detachable feet and buttoned waist, holding a handful of playing cards too large for my thin, brown fingers. I became aware of how small I looked, of how small I was, saw those eyes became sad. I knew the apocalypse had started before he said her name.

"Dorothy."

"What? What did she do now?" Grandma threw her cards on the table. It sounded like an open palm slap. She was standing, her voice beginning to shake. I knew then that she knew, too, could read the obituary listed in Travis' eyes.

He took a step back towards the door, back away from his mother's heavy steps, away from the orphan in his pissy pants. He pointed behind him, over his shoulder at the door. "Down at Langlade's." He took another backward step. "They already called the priest."

"Nooooo!" Grandma fell to her knees, an alarmingly aggressive movement in an old lady. Her hands clawed at her blouse as if she would rip open her own chest and tear out her broken heart. I watched her from my chair, where I sat. My cards, having fallen from my numb fingers, were floating in the yellow puddle around my knees.

After the funeral, I went to stay with my mom's best friend, a six-foot Cree I called Auntie Dave. My uncles were too busy drinking and getting kicked off the reserve for increasing the population. Grandma never was really the same and, even if she had been in her right mind, child services thought her apartment was too tiny for a growing boy and an old woman. At that time, my dad was still AWOL. Besides, my mom would have wanted it that way; she was always keen on me spending time with Auntie Dave. Clearly she knew I was gay before I knew what that even meant. I wonder if she also knew about Dave being magic? I didn't, not until my seventh birthday.

Dave's place was what my mom called 'beauty in the eye of the beholder; crap in the eyes of the town.' It was up on the hill behind St. Ann's where my mother was buried, and set back from the road by an acre of wild flowers and tall grass. You had to turn off onto a dirt road that wound into curves and one cheeky loop for no apparent reason, and follow it all the way to the line of birch trees that stood as slim sentinels to the actual home. The place looked like abandoned vacancy from the road. But behind the birches was a kingdom.

The house was three stories high with a sloped roof like the red pagodas of Japan. The back was bare but the front looked like a patchwork quilt of glass and frame. No less than thirty windows of all shapes and sizes were plugged into the front, giving thirty different views of the pond and the bush and the shed, that just happened to be an honest-to-god library instead of a place to keep tools and camping gear. The trees here were strung with little white Christmas lights and there were three different hammocks hanging from the low branches on the opposite side of the pond like multi-coloured cocoons hung with string-work lace.

Auntie Dave slept in a loft on the third floor. It was a huge space that included a small bathroom and a desk piled high with paper, books, bottles, scrolls and a magnifying glass so substantial I couldn't hold in in one hand until I was ten years old. His space was crowded but tidy; braided rugs strewn over the floor, stain-glass Moroccan lanterns hung low from the slanted ceiling, and a rack of deer antlers across one wall that held his silk kimono, a knitted toque from old Nunavut and a vintage champagne-coloured gown heavy with glass beads and crystal finishes.

"Some days you need to feel like a young Catherine the Great, even out in the bush," he had explained.

Auntie Dave gave me the downstairs bedroom on the second floor, off the living room. The first floor was taken up by a bathroom, the kitchen with its glass cupboards and slate island, and the dining room of regally mismatched chairs with a chandelier crafted from branches and small bulbs. The whole house was whimsical and unexpected and I loved it.

My room was small by comparison, but the biggest I'd ever had. There was already a four-poster bed against the wall, hung with red velvet curtains and with a soft globe lamp hanging on the interior. The dresser was so large, all my earthly possessions fit in one-and-a-half drawers. I used the other two-and-a-half to keep my growing rock collection, and later, to house the catalogues and magazines that captured my interest in a way that made me want them in my room, near the bed.

I slept for a week straight after they buried my mother. Dave let me be for the first three days, but then started waking me up to eat on the fourth, and by the fifth, had devised chores that I must get done before I could hole-up in my bed with the curtains drawn tight.

"Can't wait for things to change. You need to move them along yourself. Sometimes the best way is with work," he'd say, handing me a shovel to move the snow off the library path. "Just to the library. I'll take care of the other path."

The other path was a bricked laneway that led away from the back of the library and into the woods. I assumed there was an actual tool shed back there. Or maybe a woodpile. Mostly I was just grateful I didn't have to shovel it and didn't bother to ask questions that might lead to it being on my 'to-do list.'

By early spring, we were eating two meals a day together at the round, wood table on the bottom floor. Dave cooked, which was new for me: chicken and Fruit Loops for brunch; spinach and fresh bread for dinner. It was as if he wasn't sure how to put things together in a normal kind of way. I wondered if other people ate this way.

"Well, it's your seventh birthday in a week." He said this over pancakes and celery on a sunny May morning.

I nodded.

"Seven is an important number."

I blinked.

"Time to start again. It's a new cycle."

He nibbled a celery top, pulling off the tiny leaves and chewing them with his front teeth, white and green against his dark skin.

"Next week we go into the bush." It wasn't a question. He left the table and I finished my meal, stuffing strips of pancake into the hollows of my celery.

I woke up early on the morning of my birthday, brought to consciousness by sounds from the kitchen. I walked down the stairs to Dave in the champagne gown, long hair unbraided and wavy across his back like a dark habit.

"Happy born day, kid," he sang out, tossing a black wave back over his exposed shoulder. He danced over to the stairs and lifted me off the bottom step, waltzing me across the tiles and depositing me in the largest of our dining room chairs. I giggled, waking up completely in the midst of this small celebration.

"Auntie, why are you dressed up?"

He blinked extended eyelashes at me, carrying over a full chocolate birthday cake with a tea light on top for breakfast. "Because, boy, today is the day we go into the bush."

I blew out the candle and wished for nothing short of magic.

I draped a blanket over my shoulders, fastened into a cape by a safety-pin at my neck. Auntie Dave held my hand, his bracelets like wind chimes near my ear. We were on the other side of the library, at the top of the second path. He carried a basket with him, stuffed to overflow with carrots from our newly-sprouting garden.

He took a deep breath and we started our walk. As we walked, he told me a story.

"The generation before last were the final people to live on Old Earth. The water had flooded the lands and was poisoned by the work of man."

It was the migration story, of how we came to New Earth a hundred years ago. I'd heard it many times in my youth. All kids do.

"Indigenous people, we were hit pretty hard. Not only did we lose our land, but we were the last to be evacuated to New Earth. A last priority. By then, so many of us had died and so much was lost."

The trees out here were dense. The lower branches grabbed wisps of Dave's hair so that he looked like a mad queen in his gown and hair crown. We ducked and untangled and kept on the path.

"We were careful about what we brought with us. We weren't allowed much, so the Elders held Council in nations across Turtle Island to decide what was best, what was integral to our survival.

"Every nation had priorities and those were carefully listed and collected: species of fish, weirs, ulus, quilt frames, seeds for sage, tobacco, cedar, plantain, dandelions, sweetgrass, a hundred strains of corn, and so on. Everyone decided to take as much of the lands that were left and crates of dirt were scooped up and stacked in our ship, labelled with the original names of the territories from which they were pulled."

I listened, but was more interested now in what was ahead. I'd heard as many versions of the migration story as there were tellers. Everyone put their own emphasis on the parts they thought most important. I was fascinated by the larger trees back here, the birch and willow that had been transplanted by Grandma's parents when they were given this territory for the Anishnaabe Metis.

"Do you know what the Two-Spirits brought?" Dave slowed down. We had to push our way through denser brush now.

"Two-Spirits held their own council?" This was new information. I knew about Two-Spirited people: the people who held both male and female genders, but not a separate Council.

Dave nodded. "At times we have to meet separately, when we are not at the bigger councils." He let go of my hand to hold up the hem of his gown as he stepped over some ferns.

"We met and decided on a few necessities for our people's wellbeing. And we decided on families to carry out the task of keeping them safe for the next seven generations. My family was one of them."

We came through the last cluster of brush and trees bursting with new leaves and stepped into a clearing dotted with early wildflowers and smelling strongly of sweetgrass. There was a shuffling near the back of the clearing. I strained my eyes, but the sun was so strong and all I could make out was brightness among the brown and grey trunks.

Auntie Dave bent to the side and placed the basket of carrots beside his right foot. Then he turned to me, placing a smooth hand on each shoulder. "Dorothy left us all a great gift when she had my name put on your birth certificate."

I was shocked. What about my father, the short man with the buzz cut who smelled like whiskey and old laundry? I'd met him only a handful of times, but he was always reminding me that he was my dad and should be respected as such.

"It meant that if anything happened, you would come to me, thank the Jesus. It also meant, that on paper and in spirit, I had a son." His eyes grew soft under their purple lids.

More shuffling, and a loud sniffing. I looked back across the clearing to the bright spot. I couldn't trust my sight, not with what I was seeing.

"Do you know about the White Buffalo prophecy?"

I nodded, eyes still fixed on the smooth white flank visible through the leaves.

"Did you also know that the White Buffalo holds a special place for us? They say that if you see a White Buffalo in a dream then you are truly Two-Spirited." He picked up the basket, turned back to the field and clicked his tongue.

Out of the trees came two huge buffalo, so pale they looked constructed of cloud and chalk. Following behind was a small calf, clumsy on its legs, eager in its gait. Dave walked to the centre and unloaded the basket of bright orange carrots onto the grass, his champagne gown pooling at his feet like liquid metal.

"We are the keepers of the White Buffalo on New Earth. I was the last before your mother took that snowmobile to heaven." He discreetly made the sign of the cross, touching each bare shoulder and ending at his red lips. He stroked above the nose of the female that was nudging the vegetables with her snout. He turned to me and held out one manicured hand, "Come."

I walked into the clearing with a weight much different than the one left by my mother's death; a weight that balanced out the ache and made the ordinary extraordinary.

•●•●•●•

PERFECTLY YOU

by David A. Robertson

EMMA WAS IN A ROOM that explicitly reminded her of a hospital. The walls were canvas white, and the floors as well; waxed to such an extent that when she looked down she could see her own reflection: raven black hair, coffee-and-two-creams skin, irises such a dark shade of brown that her pupils were nearly lost in them, and all of this in contrast with the room's stark décor. There was a fluorescent light flickering down on her and Dr. Samuels, the psychiatrist who had been running her through a personality test, and he and the lights and the white *everything* were contributing to a worsening tension headache. She'd been feeling impatient, and now she was ready to leave altogether, and screw the contest she'd entered on a whim—and subsequently won.

Dr. Samuels' line of questioning was interesting at first, when they were going over the reasons why she'd entered the contest in the first place, because she got to talk about Cassie, and her friends were sick of hearing her talk about Cassie, especially because she'd barely known Cassie, and the fact that she hadn't known Cassie for longer, or at all, was completely Emma's own fault.

But eventually Dr. Samuels starting asking questions like the one he did now:

"If you saw a kitten stuck in a tree, would you call the fire department, or would you climb up and try to save it yourself?"

"Do people actually call fire departments for kittens in trees? Is that a thing?"

"Please be direct."

He had a fountain pen at the ready, salivating ink, hovering over his notepad. He wore a beige cardigan sweater and was balding and had circular glasses. The only thing he was missing was a Newton's Cradle on the also-white table that rested between them, to be a textbook-perfect psychiatrist. This amused her; it was, maybe, one of the only things that kept her here at this point.

She cleared her throat.

"Sorry. I would scale the tree with my ninja skills and rescue the kitten. The fire department has better things to do, like saving kittens from burning buildings."

"Is that a cultural trait?"

"Huh?"

"Scaling trees." Dr. Samuels checked his extensive notes, perusing what he'd written a few pages back. "You told me you were...Cree."

"I mean, I was being facetious, but that's kinda ignorant."

Dr. Samuels gave her a disapproving look, paused, then flipped back to the newest page and wrote something down regarding her response. About her attitude, she thought, although she, to be honest, really would have saved the kitten herself. Maybe that was the point of questions like this, so he could fill the pages of his notepad with so much ink that they looked like sheets of grey, because that's what textbook psychiatrists do. She decided that from here on in she would robotically answer the man, and he could shove the pen up his ass.

The notepad's pages made her think of Cassie. As Dr. Samuels continued to question her, and she provided him with perfectly logical, boring answers, she thought of the school picture she had of Cassie in her right pocket, and the phone number on the back of it. Cassie had written her number in pencil, and over time, due to Emma's indecisiveness, due to Emma's longing as she rubbed it gently with her thumb over and over again, it had become smeared and harder to read. Now the grey numbers looked like trees within a dead forest in the distance, a place that was too far to get to, and, with each passing day, farther away still.

Dr. Samuels, when his questions seemed like there was an actual point to them—not, "If it was your last day on earth, what would you want to do?"—had asked Emma about the day she had met Cassie, also the day she had been given the photograph and the phone number.

"It was at a coffee shop of all places." Then, she had lost herself in the white ceiling, and played the memory against it as though it were a movie screen, the only time the white was tolerable, even welcomed. "She was at a table by the window near the back, kinda drowning in hipsters. There was an open seat at her table, the only open seat, and I asked if I could sit with her. She said I could."

"Did you really sit with her because there was only one open seat?"

"You mean, was it some kind of galactic coincidence? Was the only open seat at her table, and she also happened to be gorgeous?"

"Yes. Would you have sat there if there was, say, an older gentleman there?"

"You mean a man."

"I mean an older *person*."

"I don't know. I don't have to imagine other scenarios. She was there."

He'd asked Emma what it was about Cassie, after Emma had sat down with her because of the open seat (which she hadn't been entirely honest about, because she could've taken her coffee to go; and if it hadn't been someone she was interested in she may well have done just that). She answered that Cassie was beautiful and vibrant, but it was more than that. It was the way some of her hair kept falling in front of her face, and how she pushed it behind her ear. It was how down to earth she was, and funny. She said she'd worn a brown shirt because it really brought out her eyes. Nobody with brown eyes had ever said something like that—Emma hadn't—but she was right, too. It was how she didn't like sipping at the same area of the cup that she'd left lipstick on (the subtle shade of pink she wore), so the brim of her cup was decorated with the impression of her lips, all around. And it was how she looked at her, always quickly, like she,

Emma, was too bright to look at, and how each time Cassie looked away she kind of bit at her bottom lip.

And those were the things she thought now, and the answers she had given Dr. Samuels at the beginning of this now-excruciating interview. She had answered each one of his questions honestly, too, she thought, except one:

"Why didn't you see her again, or call her, if you feel like this now?"

"I don't know."

But she did; she just wasn't sure if she wanted *him* to know, if she wanted those words lost in the thundercloud of his notepad, or if it would hurt too much for her to verbalize it. Thinking about the promise of them, of her and Cassie, sitting feet away from each other, separated by a decaf Americano, a Peppermint tea, and a small, circular table, gradually leaning closer to each other but never touching, was easier, and better.

The following week, Emma was sitting in a similar room. It might've been the same room, for all she knew. It was blinding white just like the other. She hadn't paid much attention when she'd been escorted there. Thankfully, Dr. Samuels was nowhere to be found. In his place was a technician, as she called herself, named Pyper—a tiny young woman with dyed pink and blue hair in a pixie cut, thick-rimmed black glasses, a Thundercats t-shirt, skinny jeans, and Toms (pretty much the opposite of how Emma pictured a "technician")—who presently was affixing stickers with little metal centres to Emma's forehead and temples.

As this was being done, Emma did wonder if she were, in fact, in the same room. There wasn't a table between Emma and Pyper, but rather an overbed table close to the side, on which sat a thin, silver laptop. There were wires of different colours attached to the stickers that tangled up, snaked across the bed, and connected to the laptop via a USB outlet. Emma thought the wires, twisted together as they were, looked like a messed up little rainbow. Emma herself was sitting in a cushioned reclining chair that should've been comfortable, but wasn't. She'd been squirming, which, in turn, caused a very patient Pyper to adjust the odd sticker. After the latest adjustment, she asked Emma if she was okay.

"I feel like I'm at the dentist, only you've got stickers, not fluoride."

Pyper put one last sticker on Emma's right temple, and then sat back in her own chair, and folded her hands across her lap.

"Well, the good thing is that, once we actually get going, you'll be in this chair for less time than getting a fluoride treatment."

Pyper slid the table over, right against her stomach, and started typing on the laptop quickly and precisely. Emma thought it looked like she was playing the piano. As she conducted a concerto of keyboard taps she carried on their conversation seamlessly.

"Do you like peppermint or strawberry?"

"Huh?"

"Fluoride. What flavour do you get?"

"Oh. Peppermint. Always."

"That's my favourite tea."

"Really? I like coffee. Americanos. But decaf. I can't handle caffeine."

"You don't say." Pyper looked away from the laptop, towards Emma. "It's good for digestion. Peppermint."

"I've heard that before, from—"

"Cassie, right?"

"Yeah...right."

Emma had, indeed, heard it from Cassie. She'd asked Cassie why she, like her, wasn't drinking something more complicated and befitting of the coffee shop they were in. This was something she'd discussed with Dr. Samuels, but had Pyper memorized the novelization of their interview? Was it on her laptop right now? What was on her laptop, and what was she typing?

"You know a lot about me, you know, and I know exactly nothing about this...

"Vacation."

"...vacation, right. Just to clarify: I'm the first person who's tried it?"

"Specifically," Pyper carried on with her typing, "the first person who doesn't work here to try it, yes. But I've done it. I designed it, so I sort of had to. I'm the guinea pig."

Pyper raised her arm to concede that she was, in fact, the guinea pig, and did so, it seemed, without breaking stride in her typing. Impressive.

"And you're fine, right? You look fine, so you must be fine."

"I'm fine. Really."

Emma still had the picture of Cassie. She had it out of her pocket, pressed between her right palm and thigh. Cassie's phone number was undoubtedly getting even more obscured by this action, the numbers slowly, but assuredly, evaporating into a cloud of dust. To calm herself, because at this point she felt relatively certain she was about to have a panic attack, she did two things: she recited Cassie's number over and over in her head, as one might count to ten in order to calm their nerves, and she thought about Cassie's picture, because it had always struck her, not only because Cassie was gorgeous, but it *looked* like her. To Emma, school portraits were like passports or driver's licences or her own Status card: they took a person's face and made it look like that same person's twin. The uglier, grumpier, fraternal twin. When Cassie had given Emma the wallet-sized photograph, because she couldn't find a paper on which to write her number (which Emma was fine with. She had stared at the photograph every day since), Emma held it up beside Cassie's face and said, "It's you. It's so perfectly you."

When they (and Emma still wasn't sure who *they* were; one of the many curiosities which were now flooding her brain all at once) had asked for a picture of Cassie so they could build a "virtual composite" of her, Emma thought that whatever version of Cassie they built, created from the romanticized version of her that Emma had provided to Dr. Samuels or not, it would at least *look* exactly like the Cassie she longed for.

"Tell me how it works again." Emma no longer felt as though her heart might explode out of her chest and paint the walls red in some Jackson Pollock kind of way; the number-reciting and Cassie-picturing had worked, but she still felt the need to know what she was getting into.

"Okay, well, forgive me if I give you the layperson's terms." Pyper stopped her typing and once more turned her attention to Emma. "Essentially, we're going to make you dream, but the dream is going to feel completely real, and you're going to dream for a very long time..." she stopped for a moment, as though figuring out how she could explain everything, and if she were doing it properly to begin with. Finally, she continued: "...to you. It'll feel like a long time to *you*. But, in reality, it'll be a few minutes at most."

"How long do I get to spend with her?" Emma sat up a bit from her chair. "How long will it feel like?"

"Years." Pyper leaned towards Emma and eased her back into a sitting position. "Possibly."

"And how do I, you know, get out?"

"You'll leave when you're ready to leave."

"But how?"

"If I told you the surprise ending of a movie, before you actually watched the movie, would it be as good, as fulfilling?"

Emma thought of watching *The Sixth Sense* at the urging of her father, and knowing Bruce Willis was a ghost from the beginning, thanks, also, to her father.

Truth.

"I guess not."

Pyper nodded, and then returned to her typing. "Part of the journey is the ending. It's the whole experience. You'll know when it's over. That'll have to be good enough."

"Okay. Okay, fine."

Pyper stopped her flurry of typing, really it was something to watch, with a bold strike to one key on the keyboard.

"Ready?"

Emma swallowed hard, and then took a deep breath. She nodded quickly, wanting Pyper to get it over with just as quickly.

Pyper checked her watch, marking the time. "It is now 10:34 in the AM. Starting vacation for client Emma Bear." She turned to Emma. "Here we go."

Emma saw Pyper slide her finger in one motion over the laptop's trackpad, and then tap it gently. Immediately after this poetic movement, Emma felt a surge of pain in her skull, starting at the stickers fastened to her head, moving its way through her brain, behind her eyes, and then out across her entire body, as though the agony were mixed in with her blood.

She screamed.

She heard Pyper shouting over her screams.

"Not good! So not good!"

Then, over the searing pain, over her screams, the pain ended as quickly as it had come, and everything white turned black.

When Emma woke up the pain had dulled into an ache, and though awake, she didn't open her eyes at first. Rather, she tried to ease her way into consciousness, noticing first that she was now supine, lying on a bed with cool sheets that felt like a burlap sack. The room was cool, too, but it wasn't unpleasant. And wherever she was, it was bright. She saw red and tiny blood vessels through her eyelids. She worked hard to open her eyes; they felt glued shut. When the world came into view for the first time, everything was white again, as though she had woken up in the middle of a blizzard. She heard quiet footfalls leading away from her, and a whisper.

"She's awake."

There was rustling outside of the room, which Emma realized quickly was a hospital room, even though, to this point, she had only been looking upward. It was the feel of it, and the smell, like sickness washed with bleach. She could see the ceiling, the light fixture (switched off), and a window against the right wall. She could see that the sky was blue and cloudless, and there was a dream catcher hanging in front of the window, rocking hypnotically. Its shadows fell across her body in the pattern of webbing.

Somebody entered the room from Emma's left, and she struggled to move her head to face that direction. Her neck muscles weren't keen on cooperating. Eventually, she did move her head enough to the left so that it kind of fell into place against her pillow. A nurse had come to sit with her, had pulled a chair right up to the side of the bed, and had instantly put a hand against her forearm. Her touch was careful, and she had these elegant curves, doughy eyes, and soft grey hair that looked as though it might keep rising into the air like smoke. There were two people outside of the room in the hallway. They weren't in view. Emma could hear their excited whispers, and their shadows stretched across the floor, coming to a stop under the clock on the wall directly in front of her.

It was 3:47 pm.

"Don't mind them." The nurse's nametag read Maggie.

"I…" but Emma stopped. Her throat hurt, and her voice was weak and laboured.

"Try not to say too much. It'll take a while to get your voice back."

Emma nodded. Maggie rubbed the inside of her forearm with her thumb. It felt comfortable. Emma looked down at the nurse's hands, and then, finally, her arm.

"What the hell."

"Don't talk, okay? Just relax."

Maggie's touch quickly became firm, as though holding Emma in place, as though she might slip away right there.

"Calm down, now. It's okay, Emma."

Emma mustered up the strength to pull her arm away from Maggie's hand, and held her own hand in the air so she could see it clearly. She didn't recognize it. It was pale, almost as pale as the walls surrounding her, veins were protruding like tree roots, and her skin looked like it might slide right off her bones. She held up her other hand, as though to see if it matched, and it did. She turned them methodically, from front to back, and repeated this movement for what seemed an eternity. She heard the nurse sigh.

"You were in an accident." Maggie reached towards Emma's left hand, but Emma let her arms fall at her sides, avoiding any comfort. "A virtual reality program, years ago. You went into a coma."

"How many years?"

Maggie cleared her throat. "It's been sixty-eight years. You're eighty-five now."

Emma's heart started to race. She tried to get up, but could only raise her head inches away from the pillow. She began to roll away from Maggie, to the opposite side of the bed, but Maggie stood up and held her down, and then sat beside her on the bed and stroked her hair gently.

It was quiet for a long time. The only sounds were from Maggie, who had continued to stroke her hair and started to make calming sounds, like tiny waves against a shore; people Emma had still not seen gathered outside of her room, who maintained an intense, albeit whispered, conversation; and, now and then, the dream catcher brushing against the window. In the silence, Emma looked around the room, in an effort to settle herself down. Now that she knew her age, she realized she assuredly *felt* her age, and probably worse, because she hadn't moved on her own in six decades (although was later told that physiotherapists had kept her muscles from atrophying).

As she scanned the room, she couldn't help but notice that, here in the future, nothing seemed like it belonged in a sci-fi movie, unless Maggie was some kind of a robot. The clock, the walls, the floor, the ceiling, the bed, the chair Maggie had pulled to Emma's side, the television affixed to the top corner of the room, the door with two hinges and a metal handle—none of it would've been out of place when she was seventeen years old (which seemed only minutes ago). She inspected the room thoroughly, left to right, and eventually rested her eyes on the bedside table at the right side of her hospital bed, directly underneath the window. The table was light brown, maybe oak, thankfully not white, and there was a picture frame on it with Cassie's familiar portrait trapped behind the glass.

"What's different now?"

Maggie had been watching Emma look across the room, and how she stopped when she saw the picture. "Not much. Not really. We're still waiting for our flying cars, you know...a little hotter, maybe."

Emma nodded.

"We'd probably idle in flying cars, too."

"We're kind of clueing in now. Took forever."

"Sixty eight years or so."

"Or so."

Emma lifted her arm, and almost in slow motion reached to her right and picked up the picture. She placed it across her chest, and held it steady with her boney fingers. Maggie smiled at that.

"Somebody invented these, I guess, hologram pictures once, instead of actual pictures."

"Oh?"

"So, you'd walk through a hallway and people would be standing around, people who would've been in picture frames, on walls, before."

Emma didn't respond. She imagined it, though, how it would feel to see Cassie standing at her bedside now, seventeen years old. But Emma would be an old woman lying in bed, a sack of flesh and bones. She quickly banished the thought.

"People like pictures. They like pictures and they like books. We'll always like those things, I think."

"Yeah."

"Sometimes it's better to hold the actual thing in your hands."

Emma nodded and a tear fell from her eye, as though she had shaken it loose. The tear slid down her cheek to her chin, dangled there for a moment, then dropped and landed in her jugular notch, and stayed there. She placed her thumb against the glass, over Cassie's face, and rubbed it back and forth gently.

Maggie moved off the bed and sat down on her chair, sensing that Emma would need some space. "She comes here, once in awhile."

Emma looked away from Cassie's picture, as quickly as she had moved since waking up, as quickly as she was capable of, towards Maggie.

"What did you say?"

"She comes here. She reads to you. She smudges you, said your parents taught her that once. And sometimes, you know, she just sits with you."

"Did you say 'comes,' not 'came'?"

"Comes. Once in awhile."

"How did she know I was here?"

"She said that when all this happened, your parents, they knew about her..."

"Of course they did. Everybody did."

"...and they got your stuff. They got that picture of her *with* your stuff. And they called her. The number was on the back. So, she came, and she comes."

"How often is once in awhile?"

It seemed like an eternity before Maggie responded. She looked up towards the ceiling, at nothing, as people do when trying to recollect information, and it made Emma think that Cassie hadn't been all that often, and if she hadn't, why had she, Emma, gotten so excited. But in a moment, it didn't matter, because Cassie had been here at all, and came still. So, as Maggie opened her mouth with a response, "once in awhile" and its inherent vagueness didn't matter all that much.

Maggie, it seemed, had made that same determination.

"I could call her for you. Of course I'll call her for you."

Emma turned the picture frame around, and, with her old and tired fingers, fumbled with the four latches on either side of the frame. She opened the back of the frame and took out the picture. She looked at Cassie's picture as though she had only just discovered it, and then turned it around to the phone number written in pencil, the numbers preserved, still barely legible. But legible.

"Okay."

The next day, Emma was sleeping, dreaming about something that, upon waking, she wouldn't remember or care to recall, when she was stirred awake by the sensation of her mattress decompressing. She was turned away, facing the wall, and when she opened her eyes they came to rest on Cassie's portrait. Cassie, seventeen years old, with brown eyes, olive skin, and sandy blonde hair. She remembered the first thing she'd said to Cassie, decades ago, after sitting down across from her. "Your hair reminds me of the beach." It seemed so damned cheesy at the time, so frustratingly awkward.

"Tansi."

The voice was weathered, cracked, but Emma knew it was Cassie. She turned onto her back, and was met instantly with Cassie's smile. And for the first time since she'd come out of the coma, Emma smiled too.

"Where'd you learn that word?"

"Your parents taught me some words. They wanted me to say them to you."

"You knew them? My parents?"

Cassie nodded.

"I knew them well. When they got older, I used to pick them up and bring them here."

Emma shook her head.

"You knew them longer than I ever did."

She started to cry. The last time she'd seen them, she'd lied to them. She said that she was going to school, but really she'd gone to that little white room, and now they were dead. She felt tears fall from her eyes, run down her temples, and disappear into her hair, onto the pillow. Cassie dabbed at Emma's eyes with a tissue. Emma thought of the coffee shop, how after her brilliant first words to Cassie, she'd nervously spilled some decaf Americano on the table, and Cassie had wiped away the little drops of brown liquid in the same way, as though she were practicing for this moment, right now. Emma looked at Cassie, from her delicate fingers all the way to her face, and she could see Cassie, the Cassie she had met so many years ago, even through looser skin, wrinkles, blemishes, but mostly in her eyes. She looked at Cassie's portrait, to her wide brown eyes there, as though surprised by her own joy, then back to the real Cassie, and then, with effort, reached up and put her hand against Cassie's cheek.

It was the first time they touched.

"It's you. It's perfectly you."

For the next few weeks, Emma was happy to see Cassie every day.

"Is this more than once in awhile?"

"Yes, but not that much more."

Cassie told her that she could come as often as she liked, and she liked to be here. She'd said that she, like Emma, hadn't anybody left. Her wife had died years earlier.

"Would you come anyway, even if I was well?"

Emma had asked this once, knowing that even as she'd just woken up, she was fading back into a "more permanent" coma. "The forever kind." That's what she'd said specifically.

"Yes."

Cassie would talk, mostly. Emma never had much to say because her life had passed like a dreamless sleep. So Emma would listen, mostly. She would listen to Cassie's life. Sometimes, she'd imagine what her life would've been like if she'd stayed awake.

"Do you think if I hadn't fallen asleep we would've never seen each other again?"

"I don't know. That was up to you."

"I know, I'm sorry."

"We don't need sorries now, Em."

"I'm glad I slept, then. If I can't be sorry."

"I'm glad you woke up."

"Yeah, me too."

On the day Emma died, after most of their time had been spent with Cassie reading to her, and though talking had become more and more difficult for Emma, Cassie asked what she said she'd wanted to ask for over sixty years.

"Why didn't you call?"

Emma started to answer, but couldn't. Her mouth and lips were too dry. It felt like they were made of stone. Cassie reached to the bedside table, where beside the picture of her there was a Dixie cup half full of water, and a small pile of Q-tips beside it. She dipped a Q-tip into the water, and then ran the wet cotton across Emma's lips.

"I loved you so much when we met. I kept thinking how much it would hurt if I lost you, if I only kept loving you more."

"You're a silly girl."

They didn't say another word to each other, just looked at each other, and it wasn't more than an hour later that Emma's eyelids started to shut, no matter how hard she tried to keep them open. It wasn't frightening, though. It felt no different than if she had simply stayed up too late, and her body was telling her that it was time she got some rest.

She blinked once, twice, and then her eyes stayed closed.

She heard a muffled voice. *Angels?* she thought. It was bright. She saw red through her eyelids, and could've counted the tiny blood vessels, if she had the patience. She struggled to open her eyes. They felt glued shut. When she did manage to open them, she could only see blurred white at first. *Heaven?* she thought. *Is this heaven?*

"It is now 10:36 am. Just relax, Emma. Take a deep breath. You're going to feel weird for a moment."

"What happened?"

"You're done. You're out."

"Out?"

Gradually, the room came into focus, and Emma collected her bearings. *Out*. Back surrounded by the white walls, in the dentist's chair staring up at the white ceiling, not dead, not somewhere in the sky surrounded by clouds. That, at least, was a relief. She'd never believed heaven was like that. Pyper, who was still sitting at her side, pushed the overbed table away. It rolled a few feet, and then stopped. She smiled at Emma reassuringly, as though to say, yes, you're out, you're okay.

"You okay?"

"I think so."

She leaned forward and squeezed Emma's hand, then let go.

"Can I get you anything? Water?"

Emma licked her lips. They were dry. She wished Cassie were there, that she would run a wet Q-tip along them again so she could speak. She could feel Cassie's portrait framed within her palm.

She thought of her own school picture, and her fake smile and the deep water background that the photographer had put up behind her, like she were smiling while drowning. How did Cassie remember her? Did she have a perfect image of Emma, like Emma's perfect picture of her? She lifted her hand—light brown, smooth skin, tight against her bones—and began to flip Cassie's picture from front to back, front to back, until settling on her pencilled-in phone number. Did Cassie think of her at all? Was she waiting, right now, by a phone, hoping that Emma would call? Did she walk by the coffee shop almost daily, to see if she could catch a glimpse of Emma, just to *see* her, if nothing else, as Emma had done?

Emma would imagine them there, sitting at their table alone in the crowd, the steam from their drinks mixing together and dancing in the air, talking about all the things they had done apart from each other, and the things they might do together. One day, the phone number would rub away. But that didn't matter. She'd memorized it, and would never forget it.

The End

•●•●•●•

THE BOYS WHO BECAME THE HUMMINGBIRDS

By Daniel Heath Justice

THIS IS A TEACHING, AND A REMEMBRANCE.

In the far ancient days, when the boundary between worlds was thinner, and when transformation was an everyday truth of the world, not a doubt, a strange boy lived in a dying town. Food no longer nourished the People, who sat listless and grim in the shadows, hiding from the parching sun. Unhealthy waters flowed sluggish and mute in staining colours of orange, red, and brown. Plants had long ago withered and blown away, when the People thought the drought was at its worst, before it worsened further. The only beings left to share the town were half-starved dogs and half-mad wildcats who had no place else to go. It was a place of daily cruelty, where laughter was only mockery, where touch was meant to hurt, where beauty went to die.

Though young, Strange Boy had heard the whispered tales, and he knew that once, long ago, beauty had lived there, too, long before the People had turned against the world, one another, and themselves. He caught flickering glimpses of that beauty in the rainbow shimmer of oil on the water, in the quivering hope of the tail-tucked puppy, in the sunset silhouette of a dead oak on the horizon. He believed that renewing that beauty was what would bring a healing to their world. It was the only thing that could.

So he committed himself to the task, though he knew it would be a challenge. When others trudged to their daily labours, Strange Boy danced at their side, until their rage forced him to flee. When their voices went mute or grew fierce, he lifted his shaky voice in song, until he was shouted down or cuffed into silence. He carefully gathered bright pigments from hidden places and used them to dye his rough cloth into hues long unseen by eyes grown weak from disinterest; he returned again and again to that secret spot even as his once-radiant clothes were bespattered with shaming filth. Every defiant day brought him down from the hills in his bright rags and uncertain steps and trembling song, and every night found him alone in hidden places nursing fresh wounds, weeping for the beauty that gave balm to his breaking heart, the beauty that the People so fiercely refused.

There were some moments of possibility, when the barest hint of a smile crinkled an elder's sun-dry lips, or when a group of children, once sullen, hummed a few chords of his song, feeling something of its rhythm before others screamed them back into mute hate. And occasionally he found a companion in the welcoming darkness, all insistent arms and moist tongue and firm flesh, but the night's delights never lasted until morning, and he always awoke alone. The fleeting glimpses of what could be were the only thing that kept him trying, for he knew that there was something beyond the unhappiness of the now.

One day, the People had enough. Strange Boy had once again painted over his many bruises, wrapped cunningly woven bandages on his wounded flesh, and danced with only a slight limp into the town, only to face a wall of cruel, hating smiles awaiting him. Their judgment was swift. He was stripped naked and beaten again; the paint was scrubbed from his flesh until he bled; his meagre belongings were broken, his name taken away. The crowd dragged him to the limits of the town and forbade him to return.

In those times, as now, to be exiled was to face death—slow or quick, the end was certain. Strange Boy returned to his hidden place, where he lay sobbing in fear and unspeakable loneliness. The last flickering spark of hope was fading. At last, he had been driven to the thin edge of despair.

And then a sound outside his sanctuary caught his attention, and he looked up to see a familiar young man from the town standing shadowed in the rock archway. They were not strangers, these two. Strange Boy had always admired his visitor's quiet manner, his dimpled cheek, his bright eyes. They had shared more than one brief, tender moment in the shadows, but in the subsequent daylight the one he called Shadow Boy had stood in silence as the crowd inflicted its cruelties. They now watched each other warily for a long time, saying nothing, until at last the newcomer stepped inside and knelt with a bowl and a cool, fragrant cloth that he used to wipe away the blood and the mud and the pain. His voice was low, almost without sound, and asked for forgiveness for his cowardice that day and for all the days before. He whispered of his fear, of this moment together, the sun high above, and what it would mean for the rest of his life. Then he spoke, louder now, of his longing for the gentle beauty that Strange Boy had so often and generously given to the People. And as his words poured out, their two hearts fluttered together like bird wings in flight. Strange Boy reached out, and this time Shadow Boy did not pull back. He met Strange Boy's touch and they embraced. And in the flowering of this loving moment, their bodies began to change. Scarred skin became bright feather; brown eyes darkened black; sable hair brightened to iridescent green and scarlet and turquoise.

Now they rose up into the air and danced, together and apart, then together again, flashing through the air with dazzling colour and the whir of beating wings. They danced until they were exhausted, found sustenance in the bright fierce flowers that still endured in hidden places, then danced again. The loneliness that Strange Boy had known was now gone; the solitude that Shadow Boy had long reconciled himself to was now memory. They were two and one at once.

In the days that followed the Hummingbird Boys sped through the air in mutual harmony, delighting in one another's company and movements; each night they returned to their human bodies to share different, more earthly pleasures. And although they chose hidden places for their nightly enjoyments, in the daylight they flew with graceful abandon, unaware of the dust-rimmed eyes that gazed skyward.

But gradually they learned that their shared song was not the only new sound in the world. There was another—a deep, rumbling groan that grew in intensity with every day that passed. Late one afternoon, as the hot sun crept toward the horizon, and when curiosity was too strong to resist, Strange Boy and Shadow Boy returned in feathered form to the sun-baked place they had once called home. There they made a startling discovery: in their new bodies, with eyes unveiled by fear or hate, they could see the very hearts of the People. And to their amazement and joy, in every direction they looked, there were hummingbirds. Jewelled feathers of every hue shone like multi-coloured flames through shamed flesh and unyielding bone. And the sound they heard was a chorus of captive hearts. So many luminous hearts beat like frantic wings, desperate for release but held fast by self-loathing and the fear of judgment and disregard. Strange Boy and Shadow Boy realized at last that they had never been alone. They were just the first to free their hearts and fly in their own beauty.

So they darted to those whose hearts beat strongest, streaks of blinding bright grace, calling to them in soft voices, sharing stories of possibility beyond the grim dust of what *was* to a hopeful possibility of what *could be*. And some of their kindred responded to the long-awaited call, body changing to echo spirit, becoming more themselves than they had dared imagine, rising up and out of shame to join the Hummingbird Boys, streaks of dazzling rainbow difference that lit the darkening sky. Those things that they had once been taught to hate of themselves—their gestures and voices, their sizes, shades, strength, age, even the facets of their most tender flesh—all were part of their own distinct beauty, made more lovely because it was shared with such generous delight. Together they danced in unexpected belonging, and joyful tears fell to the parched earth.

But not all the People had humming hearts. Some had hearts of harder, colder stuff; some had so crushed every hope of their own heart's escape that inner wings barely trembled at the call. Some looked at the bright birds in fear; others, disgust; others watched with ravenous hunger. Some preferred stale certainty to the unknown possibility of what freedom might awaken in themselves and others. And others heard the call, felt their heart leap in response, and were so filled with dread of discovery that they gathered sharp rocks and tossed them into the sky, seeking to destroy in others what they could not bear in themselves.

Some bright birds fell broken to the ground to be crushed by heavy feet; others were torn apart, their feathers now decorating rough rags in mocking display. Some returned to their cages, too frightened by the hate of those they had long called kin. But most of the freed spirits refused to be trapped again in a world empty of beauty. Now that they knew who they were, and what they could be, together, they turned back, their own voices loud, their shimmering plumage a beacon to those yet seeking release. Like iridescent lightning the Hummingbird Boys led the way among their earthbound attackers, and where spearing beak and soft wing struck flesh, bright flowers bloomed. Rocks in clenched hands dissolved to glittering stardust, and soon the air thundered with the defiant song of a thousand bright hummingbirds, and the world came alive again in a loving beauty too long denied.

And as that beauty returned to the People, there were still some who fled to the cold familiarity of the shadows, their eyes shut in denial of the world's renewed splendour. Others met the sight with tears, asking forgiveness of one another and the lands they had long neglected. Still others stepped forward to unfurl their own long-hidden beauty without the fear of judgment or rejection. It was a time of rebalancing, of taking account, of healing. Those who had died were gathered and given up to the stars, their journey softened by songs of mourning and dances of remembrance. Those who had been wounded were cared for and returned to wholeness. The People found courage and guidance through returning to their stories of times when they created beautiful things. They shared words of life and lineage, and committed themselves to caring for one another in better ways than they had. And the lovers who returned this gift to the People were given new names by their kindred and honoured for their courage: in flesh and feather alike, the Hummingbird Boys remained the radiant champions of the fierce, loving beauty that had restored their world.

Ever after, whenever someone heard the thrilling hum of soft wings in their breast, no matter how it came to be realized, no matter whether the quickening spirit was young or old, of all genders or none, the People now gathered together in love and welcome. For they understood once again, as they had long ago, that no one was expendable. No one was forgotten. No one's beauty would ever again be shamed. For it was beauty, and two brave, loving hearts, that had brought them back to one another.

This is a teaching, and a remembrance.

•●•●•●•

NÉ ŁE!

by Darcie Little Badger

ENAMOURED WITH PROMISES OF RED MARTIAN CANYONS and a hefty pay raise, I ignored the scary part about leaving Earth until I actually had to board a starship. There's nothing too risky about interplanetary space travel. In fact, it's rather mundane; passengers relax in stasis for nine months. I just hate speed. Won't ride a roller coaster. Won't bungee jump. Won't even hop off a diving board.

No drop can outrace the ascent outta Earth.

Security wasn't making things easier. The pre-boarding screener found my pills. "What's this?" he asked, plucking a rattling tin from my jacket.

"Those? Acebenzine."

He squinted, probably skimming a list of drug names on his ocular screen. "Sorry, how do you spell that?"

"A-c-e-b-e-n-zine. It's for dogs. Often prescribed to reduce anxiety before routine checkups or grooming sessions."

"Are you smuggling a toy poodle in your jacket, too?"

"Acebenzine is effective on humans. Trust me: I'm a doctor."

He squinted again. "Passenger registration says you're a veterinarian."

"Yes. Animal *doctor*."

"Okay. Dottie King, DVM, you'll be unconscious during launch and won't feel a thing."

"Not necessarily. One in ten thousand people experience unintended intra-stasis awareness during the six-hour acclimation period after—"

"We can offer you human sedatives." He dropped my tin in a contraband chute and handed me a mint-sized pill.

"Much obliged." I swallowed the medicine and proceeded to my stasis pod. Tragically, it resembled a technophile coffin. An attendant secured my limbs, applied bio-monitor stickers, and snapped the lid shut, her face scowling through my porthole. It did not take long for the other passengers to settle in. The Starship *Soto* was first and foremost a cargo carrier. This trip, which carried thirty Earth emigrants and forty-one dogs to Mars, was probably more crowded with life-forms than all of its predecessors.

Not a tremendously comforting thought. Was the crew sufficiently trained? If something went wrong, would they know how to rescue thirty landborn civilians? More importantly, why wasn't the sedative working?

"Everybody ready?" chirped a speaker near my ear. "Stasis initiation. Ten. Nine. Eight ..."

I know what you're thinking: it's safer to visit Mars than the grocery store. However, midflight disasters, albeit rare, are a special breed of terrifying. If Starship *Soto* exploded between Earth and Mars, I'd go gentle into the interstellar vacuum, my body and mind slipping from stasis to death. Helpless. Thoughtless. At least, during a highway fender bender, there's a chance to react, even if the only reaction is a passionately uttered "Sh—"

"Six."

I tried to focus on a pleasant memory: our chickens, a lamb, a rooster crowing. The desert warm beneath my feet. Mother's sweet tea. Father singing in the kitchen. Our collie herding sheep. Family surname—King—painted across a tin mailbox. A coyote, his muzzle wet and red. A needle and thread ...

"Three."

Wait. *Mail.* Damn!

"Two."

I forgot to setup my forwarding address!

"One."

Sh—

—ucks.

Stasis pod spiritualism ain't what it used to be; at its height, SPS churches appeared in every major city, on- and off-Earth. Their leaders preached: the Sleep is sacred! Encounter long-dead relatives! Witness blinding white light, heaven and hell! Hear prophesies, threats, and undying voices! All praise the pod!

Of course, SP experiences are caused by altered brain activity during the stasis wake-up phase. Once scientists replicated the miraculous hallucinations with electrodes, SPS interest dropped. It was all over the news.

Despite that, I nearly praised the pod as I regained consciousness on Starship *Soto*. Through the porthole, I saw silhouettes—my parents?—standing against a brighter-than-sun light. Mom and Dad were born before nannite revolution, when itty-bitty wonderbots surged through our bodies to elongate telomeres, degrade cancers, repair DNA, and accelerate healing. In other words, my parents aged. Died.

The silhouettes waved; I tried to reach for them, but out-of-body hallucinations don't come with hands. The light intensified, and its radiance drank their bodies.

Does it always take this long?

Ten to sixty minutes.

This is an emergency! Throw water on her face!

Horrible idea, Cora.

Look! She's scowling!

Are her eyes open? Bother me when that happens.

A face peered through dimming light: brown-black hair in a tight bun. Black eyes under thick, serious-looking eyebrows. Mouth pursed with watching-a-pot-boil concentration. Skin a warm ochre brown, adult-aged: could be anywhere from thirty to one hundred years old. Either ghosts resembled starship pilots, or I wasn't actually dead. "Are you awake?" she—Cora—asked.

"Working on it." My voice cracked twice. I hadn't felt so thirsty since the water crisis of '09.

"She's awake! Can I take her?"

My pod was open, my restraints unlatched. None of the other passengers had been roused from stasis; the only person there besides Cora was a peeved-looking man with a virtual reality headset around his neck.

"Wait," he said. "I'm checking vitals. Get her water and explain the situation."

"Sorry," Cora said, bounding to a water dispenser across the room. "Doctor Dottie King, we're still five months away from Mars, and the dang puppy stasis pods malfunctioned, so we got forty-one dogs barking to high Pluto, and Pete—he's the engineer—can't get things working again. So—"

"Are the dogs okay?" I climbed out of the pod; Cora put a steadying hand on my arm and handed me a water bottle. I chugged the entire half litre.

"Probably," she said, "but you should double check. And ... well, we don't know what to do! There are supplies in cargo—kibble cubes, beds, kennels, squeaky little toys—but this operation is one bad choice away from chaos."

"Vitals check out," the man said. "You're clear to leave."

I delicately removed Cora's hand as we walked out the door. "What's the staff situation?" I asked. "How many people can help?"

"Skeleton crew, Doc: just my co-pilot Lishana, Pete, and our stasis monitor, Vic'quell—you just met him."

"Can we recruit other passengers? If I recall, there are several sleeping veterinarians and med techs on board."

"Theoretically, but resources are tight—that includes space—and humans take priority."

"So the dogs will suffer if too many people wake up?"

"Right! Speaking of suffering: liquids have to be recycled. How quickly can you potty train forty-one dogs?"

"You're kidding."

"Don't worry. Pete and I will assist. Unfortunately, Vic can't be distracted. Too much of a liability."

"VR isn't distracting?"

"You noticed, huh?" She threw up her shoulders; the movement was more passionate than a mere shrug. "Blame bureaucracy. No worries. I'll do the work of two people!"

"I somehow believe you."

We turned a corner; the passage terminated at a sealed door. A thin, densely-freckled man leaned against its hand wheel. The fine creases around his mouth deepened with anxiety.

"Pete," Cora said. "I told you to wait inside animal bay. What gives?"

"It's too much," he said. "Woman, the last five minutes have made me a cat person."

He turned the wheel; as the door cracked, a flood of yaps and whines swept into the corridor. The egg-shaped doggy stasis pods had opened, exposing forty wiggling chihuahuas and a blue-eyed husky, his irises like glacial ice. The husky keened; they're a chatty breed, prone to howling, barking, and shrill vocalizations that mean everything from "pay attention to me" to "I *said* pay attention to me, damn it!"

"Move kennels in here," I said. "Cleaning and caring will be a full-time job; remember that dogs like routines. Playtime can happen in shifts of twenty animals—"

"I'm going to unpack supplies from storage," Pete said. "Good luck, Cora."

"Don't forget water dispensers!" I called after him. "Also, remember my medical supplies! Thanks! Hey, Pete? Can you hear me?"

From the corridor, he shouted, "Got it!"

"Cora?"

"Roger, Doc?"

"Who ordered the husky for a Martian settlement?"

"What's wrong with huskies?"

"They're an energetic breed."

"I dunno who bought him, but they paid handsomely; he's worth more than all forty chi-chis. With that money, I could purchase a house in the decent part of town."

"What town?" I asked. Cora had an accent I couldn't place; it was probably from off-Earth. Orbiting cities, with one foot in their founding nations and the other in the starry frontier, had a knack for cultivating unique phonologies.

"Any of them," she said. "I'm not picky."

"Right. Well, until we land, Blue Eyes will be your responsibility. Keep him close."

"Doc, no! I'll get attached and be *really* sad when we land."

"Your choice: one big dog, or forty teeny ones."

"Husky it is! What should I name him?"

"All mine will be Né łe," I said. "Dog."

"I prefer Conan. Here, boy." She unstrapped Conan, lowered him to the ground. With a shrill yawn-whine combo, he affectionately leaned against Cora's legs.

"Suits him," I said. "Time for routine checkups. Sick bay?"

"Right this way!"

I plucked a black chihuahua from his pod and followed Cora; the metal floor clanged beneath her boots and clacked under Conan's nails. In contrast, I moved silently, barefoot. Waffle-shaped ridges underfoot bit my skin. My soles had gone plush after years in compression socks and supportive clogs. I tread mindfully, afraid to stumble and traumatize the chihuahua. He huddled against my chest, squinting at the motion-activated light strips on the walls.

"This is it," Cora said. She opened a sliding door so quickly, it clanged. Sick bay had three examination tables and a tech resource centre. Sealed cabinets along the wall contained equipment and medicines. With my portable kit, I'd make do. Heartbeats are heartbeats; you can use the same stethoscope on people and dogs. It is, however, more difficult to convince a dog to sit still.

"Let the marathon begin," I said. When I carried the chihuahua to an exam table, he kicked his legs, as if treading water in the air.

"I think he's confused," Cora said.

"Not unusual for his breed. Thermometer, please!"

Forty-one clean bills of health later, Cora, Conan, twenty dogs, and I relaxed in the observation deck. Its outer video wall projected more stars than I'd ever seen before: the view behind Starship *Soto*. Among them, Earth shone the faintest shade of blueish white. Born in landlocked Utah, I rarely visited the ocean. Beaches were too crowded, windy, and hot. However, from afar, I admired the radiant sea.

"Why Mars, Doctor?" Cora asked. She was doing sit-ups, despite Conan's best efforts to eat her ponytail. I'd stopped counting her reps after three hundred and fifty. How many sit-ups could a human body tolerate, anyway? Maybe Cora had cybernetic abs. It was impossible to tell under her bulky white tracksuit.

"Eh?" I asked. "Why not?" I threw a monkey-shaped toy, and four chihuahuas latched onto its squeaky limbs.

"Where I'm from, people play the lottery for a chance to live on *au naturale* Earth."

"I didn't live on natural anything. Houston is a towering concrete behemoth. Might as well be in an orbiter."

"You could still travel, though. Visit parks. The Gulf."

"Sure."

"Mars is nine months away from all that."

"It's away from lots of things. I needed a change."

"Personal issues?" She paused mid-sit, all her attention focused on me and the blanket of chihuahuas warming my lap.

"Yeah," I said. "Especially one named Addie."

It's never easy to end a ten-year relationship, but few things are more awkward than a breakup in virtual reality. The simulated bench Addie chose for our "we need to talk" moment overlooked a forest trail that shone like the Vegas Strip. Illuminated VR ads, each tailored for my career, sauntered back and forth in the guise of pedestrians wearing sandwich boards. One blinking sign caught my eye:

NOBODY KNOWS BARB*ODIES* LIKE WE DO! PET-PRESERVER MAKES CALICO CLONES!

Clever pun.

"Sorry, Dottie," Addie said. "This conversation can't wait." Four months earlier, her company—satellite city engineering—sent her to their swanky branch on Orbiter Lux. Ostensibly a temporary position. Sadly, she loved the off-world accommodations. Me? I didn't care how many hydroponic gardens or ambient noise generators an orbiter contained; it was a scary chunk of metal. Meteoroid deflectors malfunctioned? Radiation shield weakened? Gravity failed? Baddie carried a bomb on board? Catastrophe!

"This is almost like reality," I said. Addie's VR avatar was taller and more symmetric than her physical self; I found it disconcerting. Granted, my avatar had a pair of ram horns and feathered wings.

"Did you remember to buy ad blockers?" she asked. Clearly, Addie couldn't see the street performer twirling a sign that promised: NATURAL INGREDIENTS = HAPPIER DOGS! SHEPHARD KIBBLE DOES NOT USE GMOS OR TEST TUBE MEAT!

"Mmmhm."

"It's not easy to say this," she continued. "You're a wonderful woman, but ..."

INTUITANKS COME WITH OPTIONAL FISH CAMS!

"... you've worked in every hellhole in North America, but draw the line at an orbiter? We have different priorities ..."

LEARN PARAKEET PSYCHOLOGY.

"Goodbye, Dottie."

Neon letters, halo bright, rose over Addie's head. A VR man had lifted his sandwich board, desperate to share the message: MARS NEEDS VETERINARIANS! COMPETITIVE SALARIES, INCOMPARABLE ADVENTURE! APPLY TODAY!

Bittersweet memories—Addie sharing my cream soda, Addie strumming a lute, Addie bowling, Addie kissing, Addie, Addie, Addie!—were replaced with visions of the red frontier. I imagined visiting dome-encapsulated hostels that overlooked the empty Ophir Chasma. There'd be warm earth underfoot—not Earth-earth, but close enough. Could I manage the first animal clinic on Mars? Support a burgeoning pet population? First dogs and then cats and then potbellied pigs! Goats, bison, passenger pigeons: dense flocks migrating through engineered skies. I'd build a paradise, one better than the home I lost as a child.

"Goodbye, Darling," I agreed.

Tactfully, I explained the breakup to Cora. "Addie and I had different goals in life. She wanted to live in Orbiter Lux, and I simply *can't* live in Orbiter Lux. There's no work for veterinarians! The only pets allowed are self-sustaining ecosystems: bacteria, GMO fish, and plants in sealed glass terrariums. We split amicably."

"Relationships are tough," Cora said, moving to a recliner beside me. The black chihuahua, who'd been monopolizing its plush seat, relocated to her lap. "I once dated another pilot. Great chemistry, but we were too competitive. I called it off after my third speed violation."

"That's not good for my nerves."

"They were solo missions, Doc! I'd never put a civilian at risk!"

"Just teasing." I regarded the swathe of universe projected on the wall. "You were a lot of help today. Thank you."

"Are you kidding? I'd pay to goof around with forty puppies. It's awesome! Right, Doodles?" She poked the donut-shaped chihuahua on her lap.

"You named him?"

"I named all of them."

As time passed, the daily dog routine—playtime, feeding, kennel cleaning, training, playtime, feeding, bedtime—staved off cabin fever. Cora's personality helped, too. She wasn't like the other skeleton crew. Vic lived in VR, only emerging to eat or shower. Pete did help with most dog chores, but he rarely strung more than ten words together. In contrast, Cora chatted insistently, and I wondered how she would have survived the trip without my company.

On the ninth day of doggy daycare, I finally asked, "How often do you do this?"

"What?" she said. "Grooming?" Cora combed a long-haired chihuahua, its wavy coat glistening under the tangle-proof brush.

"Interplanetary travel," I clarified.

"This is my first trip. Don't look so horrified. Lishana has nine flights under her belt. Plus, it's all autopilot until landing, and I'm great at that. See, I normally fly shuttles between Earth and Diné Orbiter."

"You're Navajo?" I said. The Diné orbiter, a spool of residential and industry modules rotating around a zero-grav core, was sovereign Navajo territory, completely inhabited by Nation citizens or their guests. Among the first space colonies, it lacked the bells and whistles of newer models. "Sturdy enough," Addie once said, "but nobody uses stacked models anymore. The gravity's unreliable. Sometimes, it's like walking on the moon, and other times, you're fifty kilograms heavier than you should be."

Cora unzipped her flight suit from neck to mid-chest; she wore a silver squash blossom necklace, its turquoise-embedded metal bright over her black tank top. "Yeah," she said. "I never mentioned it?"

"Never. Are you on the lam?"

"Nothing that exciting." She fluffed the chihuahua's cowlick and tied a pink bow around it. "I just wanted to know what a long haul feels like. The answer is: boring. Until this happened."

"Lucky emergency." Too lucky? I could accept the stasis pod failure. Dogs had never been transported to Mars before; new technology malfunctioned sometimes. But with five veterinarians on board, Cora chose me. I'm Lipan Apache, and though my tribe is markedly less centralized and powerful than the Navajo Nation, we have a lot in common. Matrilineal roots. Respect for wisdom and family. A history rife with suffering.

My expressive face betrayed me.

"What's wrong?" Cora asked.

"It's *awfully* convenient that you woke *me* up, considering all we have in common."

"The lesbian thing? I had no idea, if that's what you're—"

"No! Our cultures."

"Doc," she said, "are you suggesting that I was motivated by a burning desire to pal around with another Native?"

"Were you?"

She squinted. "Let's review your credentials. You have forty-seven years' experience with small animal medicine. Volunteered in twenty-nine urban pounds. Patients and colleagues provided glowing recommendations. You're thoroughly familiar with nannite biotech and ER techniques. There may be other vets on this ship, but you're the most qualified. That's why I chose you. Our repartee is just a perk."

"Wow. I'm sorry."

"Don't be," Cora said. "When enough people look down on you, doubt takes root. It makes you question every accomplishment and blame success on luck or favours." She zipped up the flight suit, hiding her squash blossom. I felt a flush of appreciation. A twinge of pain.

When she drew me into a quick hug, I felt her squash blossom press against my chest.

We passed evenings in the observation deck, betting our dessert rations over checkers. When Pete felt sociable, he projected movies on the wall and half-watched our game. Sometimes, even Vic joined us. There were minor setbacks. During week four, the thermal system malfunctioned, and temperatures dropped: 21 to 18 °C. I didn't notice until the short-haired chihuahuas began shivering and burrowing under their kennel blankies. Fortunately, there was an easy fix; we opened a crate of dog costumes—little tuxedos, dinosaur hoodies, superhero sweaters with handkerchief-sized capes—and they were the most fashionable dogs in space until Pete fixed the heat regulator.

After a few weeks, I forgot to worry.

Of course, that's when a real crisis struck.

It happened during a jog around Starship *Soto*. The passenger-habitable area was shaped like a spinning ring; centrifugal force grounded us. The pilot's cabin and several cargo carriers, all held steady within the gyroscope belly, were off-limits to anyone without zero-grav training.

"The simulated gravity here is just seventy percent Earth-strength," Cora said, her voice steady as we lapped the ship. "I'll be outta shape when I return home."

"Huh. No wonder I can carry so many chihuahuas at the same time." I gulped a hungry breath, already winded after ten minutes. "Mars gravity is even weaker, right?"

"Sure is. You'll feel like superwoman. By the way, will the doggy nannites protect them from bone loss?"

"They protect them from almost everything." The nannites stopped bone degradation, cancer, tooth decay, and aging. There were no parasites on Mars. No puppies, either; all pets were sterile. That said, did Mars really need a superwoman veterinarian? It would be centuries before wildlife could survive outside the domes. I'd hoped to stake a claim on prime land, but since when did being first guarantee anything?

"No wonder the Mars dogs cost a fortune," Cora said. "The ones on my orbiter rarely live past fifteen. It's too expensive to engineer nannites for them all."

"Orbiter Diné allows dogs?"

"One per family. That's how I learned to tie a bow." She jabbed a thumb at the five bow-bedecked chihuahuas who scampered after us; Conan was ahead, leading the jog. He moved so quickly, I couldn't see his feathered tail anymore. "What about you?" Cora asked, agilely leaping over a chihuahua that veered in front of her path. "Obviously, you're swimming in pets, but they belong to other people. Ever had your own?"

"Once," I said. "On the family farm, we owned chickens, sheep, and a collie named Kirby. All lost after the urban relocation measure passed." Cities were efficient; during the resource crises—no water, no food, no *space*—very few people could afford the country life.

"The U.S. government moved your family? You didn't live on a rez?"

"My tribe never had one," I said. "I'm descended from people who fought or fled the invasion. Isn't it funny how ancient history still screws us over?"

"You don't have to talk about the farm if it's a sore spot."

"I like remembering. Say, have I ever mentioned the … shoot! Look out!"

Rounding a bend in the corridor, we nearly stumbled over Conan. He lay on his side, body taut, as if his tail, legs, and head were stretched by invisible strings. "God!" Cora said. "What's wrong? Help him, Dottie!" She dropped to her knees and cradled his head on her lap. His paws twitched, and he snapped at the air, frothing. I knew the symptoms well.

"It's a seizure," I said. "Don't move."

After a scramble down the corridor, I grabbed a diazepam injector from my emergency kit and returned, wheezing and fighting through twinges of runner's cramp. As Conan twitched in Cora's arms, I shot the medicine into his leg. His blue eyes turned to me; their dilated pupils resembling two frost-dusted pits.

"Why is this happening?" Cora asked.

"I don't know."

Once Conan stopped thrashing, we carried him to the medical bay. The chihuahuas crowded our legs, squeak-yapping. "Oscar," I said. "Rosie! Snowball! Doodlebug! Shoo! Go find Pete!" Only Doodlebug listened.

"They know that he's dying!" Cora said, hugging Conan tenderly. "Dogs have a sixth sense!" She turned her head, hiding her tears from me.

"Nah. Chihuahuas are just pests. Put him on the table. He had a seizure; that's not a death sentence. If it happens again, we'll give him daily phenobarb. Easy treatment."

"I thought all Mars dogs are healthy. Is it something I did?"

"Animals aren't machines." I checked Conan's gums and listened to his heartbeat. His hips were aligned, his stomach felt right, and his eyes scrutinized my work, alert. "Life is complex in unpredictable ways, Cora. It changes and surprises." I scratched Conan behind his ears, pleased to see his tail wag. "He's healthy. Well. Aside from the possible epilepsy. Poor boy. Are you okay? Can I get you water?"

"No, thanks. I need to visit the flight deck."

"Right now?"

"His buyers must be informed." She shook her head. "They won't be happy, Dottie. Can you watch Conan until I get back?"

"Of course," I said.

Pete and I crated the chihuahuas—it was nearly bedtime, anyway—and I moved Conan to my closet-sized personal room for observation.

Though I put his dog bed on the floor, he hopped onto my narrow bunk, curling in a furry donut at the foot. "Cora spoils you," I said. His ears perked up. "What, you miss her already? It won't be long."

Actually, a knock on my door woke us five hours later. "It's me!" Cora called. "Is Conan alive?"

"You can't hear him barking?" I slipped a robe over my pajamas and opened the door. "What's the verdict?"

Cora barely managed a half-shrug. She zombie shuffled into my room and slumped on the bed.

"Come in," I said. "Make yourself at home."

"Sorry. It's bad. The buyers requested a different pup."

I turned off the ambient cricket sounds that had been chirping through my intercom and sat between Cora and Conan. "That's what I was worried about. For his price tag, they expect perfection."

"He *is* perfect." She grabbed my hand firmly. A shade darker than mine, it felt noon sun warm. "What's going to happen?"

"He'll find a new home," I said, "with somebody who loves him. Like you."

Her posture straightened as we basked in contemplative silence; Cora was probably planning his homecoming on Orbiter Diné. All the kilometres they'd jog together, all the toys he'd rip apart. When she spoke, however, the subject surprised me. "Before the seizure, you were going to tell me something. What?"

It took a moment to gather my memories. "I'm not spiritual. Don't believe in gods, ghosts, or divine retribution. It's hard enough to have faith in people. But …"

Her hand was still on mine, our fingers entwining. It took a moment, but I eventually recognized that not-quite-platonic intimacy wove our touch, and I did not want to pull away. In fact, I wanted more.

Usually, when I fell for somebody, I fell fast. Maybe that's why I hate rollercoasters. Just five minutes after Addie introduced herself, I gave her my VR ID number and thought, "If she doesn't call tonight, I'll cry!" Cora was different. Her gravity pulled me gradually, gently. Unlike the darlings in my past, I grew fond of Cora without infatuation magnifying her positive qualities. Who knows why our relationship progressed so strangely? Maybe she was special. Perhaps the yapping, needy chihuahuas stalled our romance. Either way, Cora's warm hand felt nice.

Blushing, I continued, "... something special happened when I was a child. It makes me entertain notions like destiny."

"What?" Cora asked. So told her my story.

I was eleven years old, home alone, when I heard shrill cluck-screams, the kind chickens make as they're dying. I charged outside with my baseball bat. A coyote stood beside the coop—little coop, just enough for thirty birds—with a chicken in his mouth, a white silkie that I hand-raised from the egg. The coyote stared at me. I thought of owls: bad luck, owls. They also have yellow irises, like headlights bearing down on you, a warning or a threat.

Worried that he'd escape with Silkie, I lowered my bat and said. "Put. Her. Down." Kirby always responded to a firm tone, yet I scarcely expected the coyote to listen.

Tricksters are unpredictable.

He opened his mouth, and Silkie fell onto hard-packed dirt with a cluck-shriek. Blood matted her downy feathers; something solid and ropey dangled from her belly. I screamed. Couldn't help it. With a snort, the coyote licked his wet muzzle and trotted away.

I rushed Silkie to the kitchen and placed her in the sink. Mom sliced vegetables in the metal basin, so we kept it fastidiously clean. As if exhausted by the attack, Silkie quietly allowed me to part her wispy feathers and examine the injuries, four gashes. The most serious wound had freed a loop of intestine; gently, I tucked it back inside her body. What else could I do? My parents had no money for a veterinarian house call.

Silkie thrashed once. If she moved too quickly, her innards might fall out again. She needed stitches.

I found a needle and nylon beading thread in Mom's clutter bin. We kept bacteria-kill spray under the sink; I used it to disinfect everything: my hands, the needle, the thread, even the blood-matted feathers. Silkie didn't even cluck when I rolled her over and pinched her injury shut. "It'll hurt a little," I said. "Sorry." I could feel her fluttering pulse under my fingers, her little body's warmth. The needle reflected sunlight, a glint of silver light shooting from my fingertips. I worked quickly to spare us both anxiety. Five stitches closed the wound; just minutes later, Silkie was tottering around the kitchen, clucking and ruffling her wings

Three years later, when my parents told me that I could take just one chicken to Houston, I chose Silkie. She sat on my blanket-draped lap as we left the farm, our life—all the life we could bring with us, anyway—packed in one van and a trailer. The coyote stood alongside the dirt road, his headlight eyes trained on mine.

I waved goodbye.

"That's why you're a veterinarian," Cora said. "The coyote."

"He certainly opened my eyes." I extricated my hand and grabbed a pillow, burying my face in the cotton-wrapped foam.

"What's wrong?" Cora asked.

"I'm not sure about Mars anymore."

"Why not? The domes are gorgeous."

"Because I didn't become a doctor to twiddle my thumbs. Those nannite-hearty chihuahuas don't need me like Silkie did. This was a mistake. Never make big decisions during emotional rebounds!"

"A mistake?" Cora asked. "Or—don't laugh—destiny?"

I lowered the pillow. "How so?"

"Animals have it rough on Orbiter Diné. We always need help."

"I'm not sure I belong there."

She threw up her shoulders in the passionate manner I knew well. "We have three weeks until landing. Plenty of time for decisions." Cora stood, trailed by Conan. "Goodnight, Dottie," she said.

That night cycle, I dreamed about the red desert, but home did not comfort me. I ached for company.

For Cora.

Landing an interplanetary starship is a gradual process. Sixty hours before touchdown, the gravity generator slowed. Six hours before touchdown, chihuahuas were bouncing around like they had invisible rocket boosters on their backs. "It may be time to strap everyone down," Cora said, plucking Doodlebug from the air before he smacked into the wall. "We can use the stasis pod restraints."

"I'll sedate them, too," I said. "Er. What about me?"

"Rare honour, Doc! Lishana invited you and Conan to the flight room during descent! Don't worry. We land slow."

"Unless the ship crashes."

"Hey! None of that!"

We wrangled puppies left and right, securing them in open pods. I gave each chihuahua a fond pat on the head. "Good luck," I said. "You little Martians!"

From the intercom, a voice boomed, "Three hours. Report to landing stations."

"That's us," Cora said. She hoisted Conan with one arm and helped me manoeuvre through Starship *Soto* at ten percent Earth gravity. As we passed the observation deck entrance, I paused to admire its wall. Mars, a canyon-cracked, crater-pocked ball, loomed on the projection screen. From our vantage point, there were no signs of life. No breathing green blankets over loamy continents, no white shimmer in waters thick with glinting phytoplankton.

Nothing like the view of Earth.

I made my decision.

"I want to be awake during the nine-month return trip," I said, "in case Conan has another seizure."

"And after that?" Cora asked. "Where will you go?"

"Wherever I'm needed. The orbiter sounds promising."

As we kissed, the last trace of gravity slipped away, and my feet escaped the metal ground. I felt—I was—weightless, unbound by anything but the memories I carried and the tender warmth against my lips. Cora and I parted when the intercom insisted, "Report to landing stations."

Hand in hand, we turned our backs on Mars.

•●•●•●•

TRANSITIONS

by Gwen Benaway

I AM LATE. Crossing subway lines, zigzagging through the city's underground, takes more time than I have. My Blackberry blinks red with twenty-five unread messages from work. My second phone, the one which links me to my other life, is also blinking with unread notifications. There is nothing for it but to rush to my appointment and hope there isn't anything urgent to deal with when I return to the office.

I push into the final train which will take me to the row of medical buildings and hospitals perched along University Avenue. All the seats are taken so I grab one of the metal poles near the door and hold on. I see my face in the train glass, highlighted by the reflected lights of the subway tunnel. My foundation is too heavy. I look whiter than usual, a combination of my half breed skin tone and the mattifying powder I use to set my face. Half of transitioning from a man to a woman is learning to blend. The other half is hair removal.

I finished the first stage of my transition last Fall. Now I'm working on the second stage, hormones and living full time as my chosen gender. This is why I'm heading to University Avenue in the middle of my work week, frantic and looking like a transgender ghost. They are running a new drug study on hormone therapy and need transgender guinea pigs. I signed up because they promised less side effects, lower cancer risks, and ongoing medical monitoring. I already have a doctor in the overworked clinic in the Village, but since more support is better than less, I volunteered.

The train lurches every time it reaches a stop, pushing me off balance on my heels and forcing me to grip tighter onto the railing. I feel the glances from my fellow riders. Some days, in low light and when I've had time to work at it, I can pass if I don't speak. On days like today, behind schedule and plastering my foundation on between cups of coffee at work, I'm an obvious transwoman. I tell myself I don't care what people think. If looking like a supermodel was my primary motivation for transitioning, I'd have backed out after the first painful electrolysis session.

A man on the right side of the train keeps looking at my face. He is caught between fascination and disgust. He stares at my face, drops his eyes over my body like appraising artwork, and then looks back at my face again. I know the look. It means he thinks I'm a man but he isn't sure. He is searching me for some sign to confirm whatever assumptions he has created in his mind. I keep my eyes averted, focusing on the narrow billboards running along the top of the train. Let him think what he wants. I'm too late to care.

People think hormones are a magic pill which transform you into Tyra Banks. It doesn't work like that. They can soften your skin, shift your fat storage, but at the end of day, it's makeup and lasers which help you pass as a woman. Not that passing is my goal, but it makes you safer in public if no one can tell. I'd like to walk out of my condo and not feel like I was going to end up on the news for wearing my favourite dress, the one which shows off my arms and pushes up my tits like a platter of heaven. So here I am, departing the train at Museum station in downtown Toronto, heading into a research laboratory connected to Mount Sinai Hospital. Praying they haven't canceled my appointment and don't put me into the control group that get a sugar pill. I need estrogen like a desert caravan needs a well.

Somehow I navigate the building maze and end up in the waiting room two minutes before my appointment is scheduled to begin. The letter they mailed me, along with my legal waiver, said to be fifteen minutes early, but the bored admin just waves me into one of the offices behind her desk, and tells me to fill out my intake forms when my meeting with the research lead is done. I walk onto the office, feeling like a shaved mouse about to be injected with bladder cancer cells. It looks like every office on TV, beige and cluttered with file folders and sad spider plants.

The research lead is a polite woman in her late forties. Her glasses are heavy purple resin, suggesting a glamorous artistic personality. Her brown cashmere sweater, crumb laden and smudged with makeup, suggests a life of PBS documentary and CBC Radio 1 interviews. The contrast is striking. As she leads me through a series of questions about my gender history, I find myself cataloguing the various inconsistencies in her appearance. Sensible flat black shoes imply a practical nature. A photo next to her desktop computer shows her in a tropical location with an oversized margarita and a leopard print bikini. I wonder if she has an undisclosed drinking problem, one which encouraged her to pick out the glasses and buy the swimsuit when her real personality was safely saturated into incoherence.

My friends would tell me my focus on her appearance is patriarchy in action. I imagine my non-binary friend, Sten, scold me by saying "women judging other women is how men police our bodies when they aren't present.' I agree, but in this moment, listening to her list the long line of possible effects and downstream impacts to my biology, picking out the most banal parts of the interaction is the only way I can keep my skinny latte down. When I first came out of the Trans closet, announced my transition, and started the long process of hair removal, I felt an immediate and persistent urge to vomit. I feel the same rush of energy to my stomach now.

I interrupt, coughing to push down the bile in my throat. "Look, I know about the risks. I've read the forms and research". This wasn't lying, because I had used my workplace subscription to PubMed to scour all research related to hormone therapy from the last twenty years. "Can I just sign whatever I need to sign and start?"

She blinked at me once, mentally turning off her script and moving back to real conversation. "Yes, I'm sure you have." She pauses to purse her lips and pushes her glasses up higher on her nose. "But there are unique risks with this drug. Its bioavailability is much higher than older treatments. We're not sure how it will work in human trials."

I resist the urge to roll my eyes. I smile, tight around the corners. "Sure, but the study was approved which means it's been reviewed and the animal trials had a tolerable side-effect profile. So please, if we can move on, I'd appreciate it"

She shrugs and spreads her hands. "Fine. Just stick to the dosing schedule and make sure you don't miss any of your blood work appointments." She passes me a legal waiver to initial and date. I sign it. She files it into a blue folder and passes me another form to sign, this one confirming we went through the risks and she answered any questions I might have. I sign it as well.

Once the papers are signed, she hands me a schedule of blood work appointments, a small plastic bag with pill bottles, and a paper handout with dosage times and amounts labeled in red letters. I take the pills and the appointment schedule, stuffing them into my bag, and back out of her office while thanking her for her time. She has returned to staring at her computer screen, absentmindedly waving me off and muttering about my contribution to the advancement of medical science. Screw that noise, I think, as I rush out of the research building and towards the subway. I don't care about science. I just want to get through the next stage of my transition without any more problems.

Then what? my mind asks, as I pass through the toll collector station and return to the subway tunnels. I don't know, I answer. The seats are all taken again so I stand by the doors, metal pole in the hand while people gawk at me. I don't know at all. I can only take one step at a time towards another life in another body. I will still be me, but not the me that I've known. Closer to myself, farther away from the world and its pervasive expectations. I hope the hormones kick in quickly. I want to feel the calm which some transwomen have told me about, the slowing of testosterone and the influx of estrogen bringing peace. Almost there, I tell myself, almost at my stop for work and almost to the life I've been waiting for. I pop one of the pills into my mouth and swallow with a swig of water from the thermos in my bag. Womanhood, here I am.

Work is a slow hell. Pointless meetings with mid-level managers who will never go any further, jockeying over positions and influence like drunk coeds trying to get served next at the bar. By three PM, I'm nauseous and my makeup feels like Saran Wrap on my face. My final meeting of the day isn't a meeting at all. It's an Elder's Teaching with an old wizened Anishinaabe woman from Serpent River First Nation. It's supposed to be on the seven Grandfather/Grandmother teachings, but she's a real old time elder. She took twenty minutes to open up the teaching, smudging and thanking all the ancestors in Anishinaabemowin. The white office workers looked bored and uncomfortable which she spoke in Ojibwe. The other Indigenous staff looked euphoric in her words, as if she was the Pope blessing them at high mass and they were Jesuits. I doubt anyone else can follow anything she's saying, given how few of us have kept our language.

I know some, enough to understand her prayers, so I follow along in my head. The hormone pill is burning in my stomach. I didn't check the information booklet to see if I needed to take it with food. The Elder is talking about responsibilities in communities now, male roles and female roles. She looks over at me whenever she speaks about female roles, smiling a wide Anishinaabe smile and nodding her head a little. It's comforting to know there are still traditional people who know the place of Two-Spirit people.

My family was Anishinaabe and Métis on both of my father's sides, but we weren't raised with the culture and language. Bushcraft, living off the land in Northern Michigan, was part of my grandparent's lives, but they weren't on reserve and didn't practice any culture. The most obvious sign of their heritage was the stereotypical Indian crap around their dilapidated farm house. There were dreamcatchers in the windows, little creepy Indian maiden ceramic statues, and a mantel clock with the famous "lone brave" artwork painted on the clock face. That was their contribution to keeping tradition alive.

I liked the teaching, though, despite the vomit feeling and the fact that it was running over its allotted time. People kept leaving the meeting room, saying "sorry, I have another meeting" as they slipped out the door. The Elder just nodded at them in the unspoken disapproval style of all elders everywhere and kept on speaking. When she reached the end of the teaching, the Elder lit up more sage and started another long prayer. This time, having reached the end of my mental reserves, I phased out and let her words flow over me.

That's the moment it started, the barely audible voices on the edge of my skin singing. They were singing a traditional song, the kind women's hand drum groups across the city sing, but I didn't recognize it. It was like when my coworker turned on the radio in her cubicle on the lowest volume setting to escape the detection of our bosses. The Elder prayed on and the other people in the room didn't seem to notice anything, so it was definitely only happening to me. Something with the hormone pill, I reasoned, some weird acid-like side effect. I tried to ignore and look normal for the rest of the session.

It got worse through the day. By the time I'd taken my second dose, I was having full on visual hallucinations. While walking down Bloor Street, I saw a woman in a jingle dress at the intersection with Yonge Street. She stood on the corner, staring into the distance. At first, I thought it was a contemporary art piece by one of the Indigenous activists I know. There is an old burial ground at the intersection, so it would be the ideal place for a reclaiming piece. When a business-suited man strode through her without any effect, I knew it was the damn pills.

I dreamed the strangest dreams that night. In one dream, I was spinning just above the tree line in the bush. All I could see was a grove of winter birches beneath me and a flat, grey skyline. The singing was there as well. If I was another kind of half breed, more traditional or a ceremonialist, I would have put it down to tobacco. As it was, I just wanted it to stop. After the last dream of a rummaging bear in low brush, I promised myself I would call the research study lead in the morning. Girl has no time for this bullshit, I told myself, I'm just trying to become myself, not get into any mystical drug-fuelled cultural stuff.

When I called from my office at work, ten minutes past nine AM, the research lead wasn't in. The admin passed me to her voicemail. I left a message, explaining I was having unusual symptoms and gave her my office line. I went to work, routing emails and filtering the endless stream of drivel from my coworkers. When my phone rang an hour later, I rushed to grab the receiver. It wasn't the research leader, but the Elder from the other day. She wanted to ask if I had heard any feedback from the session and when her honorarium cheque would be mailed out. I answered her questions politely but tried to get her off the phone. I didn't want to miss when the research lead called back. The singing was still present and was getting on my nerves.

After winding down about her honorarium and the teaching, the elder suddenly switched gears and asked me what I thought of the teachings about the roles of women. I froze on the phone, letting out a long "ummmm" while my mind frantically tried to make up a neutral response. "It was interesting. Very informative?" My voice trailed up on the last word, making it a question. I hoped she would jump in and go off on a new "sacred teaching."

Instead, she went right for the jugular. "You know, it's important for you as a Anishinaabe kwe to know your teachings. And the medicines and all that." She paused at the end of her statement, waiting for me to respond.

"Yes, it is important. I'm not really a very traditional kind of woman," I said, certain this would finally end the conversation. In my mind, I imagined hundreds of missed call notifications from the research lead. The elder didn't leave it there.

"Really? You seemed like one of the only ones who was listening to me yesterday. I could tell you knew some Anishinaabemowin by how you paid attention when I was praying. Where are your people from?" Great. She is one of those elders, the kind that get off on reconnecting people to their roots.

"Yeah, I know a little bit. We're half-breeds from Lake St. Clair". I used the word half-breed, not the more politically correct word of "Métis" because I figured it would throw her off.

"Well, that's good then," she paused for a second before adding, "I am conducting a sweat next Saturday up at Anishinaabe Health. You should come."

Time to end this conversation. I had been as polite as I could and I sure as hell was not going to anyone's sweat. "Thanks for the offer, but like I said, I don't really do ceremony anymore. I have a lot of other priorities going on my life right now."

"You don't need to go to ceremony to be in ceremony", she snorted, "I know what you are. What do they call it now, a transition?" She didn't wait for me to answer before continuing onward. "You know, back when we all had our language and culture, we had our own ceremonies for becoming a woman. There was a way we went about bringing you into the world as a woman. Not all the drugs and surgeries they use now."

"I'm sorry, but I am expecting another call. I'm really glad you came out and provided your teaching yesterday. Hopefully we can have you back soon." I willed myself to hang up if she didn't accept this final closing sentence.

The elder sighed on the line. "Girlie, you aren't listening to me. You must be Bear clan, so stubborn. Being a woman isn't about your body. It's about your spirit. You need ceremony to help with that, not pills." She sighed a second time, this time a little tired. "Look, your ancestors are going to find you, one way or another. Call me when you are ready to talk to them again."

"Ok, thanks. Goodbye!" I clicked the phone down and stared out the window. Everyone was an expert in my transition and wanted to tell me how to do things right. They would tell me the right shoes to wear, the perfect lipstick, skirt length, stockings, and where the best place to get my nails done was. It was helpful and supportive, but incredibly frustrating. No one seemed to understand that this was my body and my journey. I didn't need constant reminders of what I was doing wrong, especially from an elder who knew nothing of my family or me.

The phone rang again. I stared at the call display, worried it was the elder calling me back. It was the research lead. I grabbed it on the second ring and after dispensing with the politeness of the "hello, how are you?" then launched into a description of my symptoms. The research lead listened patiently but then cut me off as I started describing more of the visual side effects.

"Look, maybe you aren't a good match for this study. I'm not supposed to tell you this, but you aren't in the estrogen control group. You are in the placebo control group, so whatever is happening is not related to this study. Maybe you should contact your primary care physician or some mental health supports?" She said the last words like I was the most insane person she had ever encountered.

"Oh. Alright. Thanks for letting me know." I wasn't sure what to say next, so I just hung up. When the phone clicked down, the sound felt like it echoed through my office. I reached up and touched the space above my upper lip where a few hairs of my beard still resisted permanent removal. Outside my window, I could see a falcon dive and twist between office towers. Every day, I watch the falcon hunt for pigeons in the parking lot, but today, it felt different. As if it was a messenger from the universe or my long dead grandmother.

The elder's words came back into my mind. Your ancestors will find you, one way or another. I hate pre-destiny, but what choice do I have? If I wasn't in the hormone study, I'd have to go on the older drugs with the higher side effects. I was not going to tell my primary doctor about the hallucinations or I'd end up having to delaying my transition even further when they made me do psych evaluations. But the last thing I wanted to do was to hang out with a bunch of traditional people talking about the way things used to be.

The singing chose this moment to return. The same low voices as before, but the feeling of familiarity was stronger. I knew these voices even if I didn't understand them. I looked at the phone, still sitting silently from when I had hung up. My eyes ran across my bulletin board until I found the post-it note with the elder's contact information. I reached for the phone receiver and moved my hand over to the keypad to dial. Womanhood, here I am. Again.

•●•●•●•

IMPOSTER SYNDROME

by Mari Kurisato

AANJI ALMOST PASSED FOR HUMAN. Her gestures were natural, her eyelashes fluttered the right way, her breathing was perfect. Still, she failed to completely shed her old self. Standing in the shower, looking at the water rippling down her brown skin, she marvelled at the artistry of the details. The moles, the creases in her thighs. But her shaking hands were brightly smeared with proof of what she *really* was. What she tried so desperately to hide.

Her blood.

Ink black, swirling in the water like oil. Even though it smelled of copper, it betrayed her. Of course, she thought she'd have more time. She wasn't expecting to be attacked on the way home from the supply depot. But the Citizens who'd beat her knew she wasn't human.

She wasn't passable. Not yet.

And she had to be. Noncitizens were not allowed on the Seed Ships.

She cried, her body shaking, wasting her week's water ration to wash away the blood that poured from her nose. Ten years, thousands of treatments, and she still couldn't bleed right.

She wondered at the blood. How, aside from a colour so wrong it almost glowed, perfectly-formed vessels ruptured just so, orchestrated on a near cellular level. There was artistry in it. But it was a failure.

The shower walls flashed bright red, one of her timers going off.

No time for sentiment. Today was it. Had to be.

She washed her hair quickly as water pipes began to groan, signalling that she was almost out of time. She towelled herself off as the news views flickered to life on the dirty glass wall of the shower. Her eyes flicked over the screens; Earth's Amazon savannah was still burning, more people were petitioning for Moon projects, and Seed Ships were leaving for terraforming projects around faraway stars.

Aanji picked up the gun and started loading the cartridges. Each one cost her a week's pay, and for a Noncitizen station traffic monitor, she was paid a lot. She primed the gun, put a pain pill on her tongue, and pressed the barrel against her thigh. She closed her eyes, rolled the pill in her mouth, and prayed. Then she bit down, uploading its medicine into her mind with a crunch. At the same moment, she pressed the trigger, the echoing crack loud in her ears.

She hid under the porch, trying not scream, not even to breathe. Spiders crawled under this porch, and it smelled like a big rodent had died here, the sour sting of rotting flesh in the open air. Normally she'd never hide here. Not even when her brothers smelled wrong and were senselessly angry, but today was different. Today the Others were here. Three of them. Corpse-like skin, watery eyes, and bad, bad smells like funeral smoke. Lights flashed everywhere like blood and water. Her mother was in the kitchen, crying, her brothers and sisters and father were already gone. The Others stood on the porch, calling for her in a warbling voice filled with lies, the soft honey-sweet words alien to her, but the impatience underneath obvious.

She clenched her eyes shut and hid, not even daring to breathe. The voices of the Others came and went. She needed to pee. She was old enough now to do that by herself, but she couldn't leave her hiding place. So she kept still, frozen with fear and shame when she lost control. For the rest of her life, she would never forget that smell, the smell of her own shame and the dead rodent in the mould under the porch.

Then, there was movement. She was caught. She tried to wedge herself against the foundation wall, but the hands of the Others were huge, fast and so strong. She screamed, and her mother's screams joined her own. They were carrying her away, corpse-like hands holding her tiny body tightly.

Aanji tried not to scream. The hands of the Others still bruised her skin, and it hurt and shamed her. These hallucinations came with each injection, and they were disconcertingly specific.

The injection pain spilled up and down her leg as conversion serum flooded her skin, her muscles, tendons, and bones. Thousands of hexagonal tiles of milk-white ceramic synthflesh spread from the injection site across her leg, rising through the epidermal layer like wet bubble wrap being popped. The hexagons sizzled, interlocking before melting into place.

She gritted her teeth, putting the gun barrel to her stomach. The pain pill rode through her awareness in stages, but she was running late and didn't have time for it to take full effect. She shot another cartridge. This time, she screamed. The scrolling news on the glass wall shivered away, and a screen asking her if she needed assistance flashed, illuminating the bathroom in dull red.

"No," she croaked after a moment.

The prompt faded away, the newsglass sliding back into view. Aanji kicked the wall with her foot and the news scroller vanished, leaving her free to sob in silence. She shot herself in the chest the next time.

Her work alarm pulsed throughout her quarters. Aanji quickly emptied the rest of the injections into her body. She screamed, hissed, and shook as she scrambled out of the tiny bathroom, punching the button that disconnected the shower and toilet from her quarters. She whipped her still-stinging arm back from the door hatch as it shut with a bang, the capsule tipping suddenly as the station shifted her unit up and away from the residential area towards the transit lanes.

Aanji clung to the guide bars near her bed and climbed into the Chameleon bag she'd bought on the Undermarket. Squirming into the bag made her feel like she was crawling into the mouth of a sea wyrm, begging it to devour her. When she was all the way inside, she sealed the top and held still. The bag stiffened a moment, inflating with a series of pops. Slimy metapolymer tendrils wrapped tightly around her, weaving into each other. Some strands tightened, crushing her breasts to her chest and stealing the breath from her, others weaving musculature around her skin, lending her smaller body the subtle cues of dimorphic certainty. Curves were flattened, hidden, height was added. The metapolymer clay baked itself onto her—*no, at this point it was better to think in terms of* himself, Aanji thought.

Aanji stilled *himself* as the metapolymers forced their way into his mouth, wrapping around and into his larynx, seeping around his vocal folds, and thickening them just slightly. This part hurt the worst. In the beginning, he had to practice for months in order to quiet the urge to tear out of the fragile Chameleon bag in a flight of terror.

The process finished. The bag pushed him up. Aanji stared at himself in the mirror.

What he saw was soulless. *Herless. It* struck him like a fist to the heart. Gender for Noncits during work hours was expected to be male. While it was perfectly *legal* (if frowned upon) for Noncitizen machines like Aanji to present as non-male during work shifts, using implants to mimic an organic body and then hiding it with an inorganic chassis was a crime. But the Chameleon bag was the best of the best, usually used in assassinations and political campaigns. The body gleamed silver, features designed to be minimal.

Aanji's capsule shuddered into the transit station. The hatch that led to a bathroom moments ago now opened onto a dusty hall of metal stairways receding into the darkness of Omni station 66. Aanji inhaled deeply, striding forward.

"Halt, Noncitizen. Present identification and gene-classification!"

Aanji was not surprised at the snappy tone Perie was taking this morning. Though they were both "machines," and knew each other, Perie Smythe, or Perimeter Security Interface One Three, was all business during working hours. Today was no different, except that the hulking body of the woman Aanji once called his closest friend seemed to glow a little brighter when Aanji approached. Angry, perhaps. Aanji hoped it wasn't because of his refusal of a dinner date a while back.

"Vermis Limax, Seven Nine," said Aanji as he held out his arm. Perie grabbed it roughly, licked it with sensor scanners in her hand, and shoved him.

"Recognized. You're late, Limax Seven Nine. You'd better run."

"Yes, thank you. Have a good day, Perimeter Securit—" Aanji started to say, but his old friend had already disappeared. He did not blame her. Even though Perie technically knew where all the Noncitizens were at all times, she probably didn't consciously think about it.

After all, it'd gotten much busier lately. With the influx of humans to Omnistation 66 fleeing Earth for Mars proper, petty crime here was on the rise lately.

No matter, thought Aanji as he ran for the stairs. If he examined it too closely, he'd have to admit, in his own way, he was a criminal just like the others.

Not entirely like the others, he reminded himself. He, no, *she,* was different.

There was a brief moment where he thought about just going to work. Accepting fate. But the woman he had befriended months ago was expecting him, and today was the very last day the Seed Ship was going to be docked onstation. So he overrode his fear, and instead of going to his workstation, he rode the lift to level nine, heading for a public Virtualis lobby.

It took Aanji five minutes to get to the virt-chair and seat himself properly on the sensor pads. Looking around as indiscreetly as possible, he prayed no one would notice him in a Citizen's chair. He leaned back against the chair and punched the CONNECT tab. The chair wrapped around him, nanomaterials weaving themselves in his body, thousands of tiny bolts of lightning. He took a deep breath and died.

At least, Aanji felt like he was dying—everything was receding at a terrifying speed. His heart stopped. As he crossed the terminus from station life to Virtualis, it felt like someone had used a knife and just scraped everything out of him, until he—

There was a man on top of her. She couldn't look. She couldn't feel. She pretended to be dead. She was a corpse in a room full of bad smells. Bad sweat. Bad sounds. The only thing she could do was stare at the ceiling.

—felt hollow, like a person-shaped gourd. These dream sensations always came like a thunderclap. Aanji opened his eyes and the Virtualis command screen shimmered into existence in his vision. He lowered his sensory perception settings until everything was muffled like a warm blanket. He stayed there as long as he could, bathing in the warmth of the low-sensation world around him, having just shifted across the terminus, that indeterminable nothing.

An alert sounded, and with a growl he made his way through Virtualis' hazy layers of data, each tissue-thin wall of light its own separate world, a digital paradise for three and a half trillion people—Citizens and Noncits alike who still called the Terran star system home. He hated the way it smelled, the billowing smoke of people writ numerical, sliding from one world to the next, each person living in the system for fear of what was Outside.

Outside was the raw truth of it, the godless vacuum that burned with the cold certainty of easy death. But outside, also, a septillion possibilities, one for every star in the observable universe. Many more than that, Aanji realized, as he slid between digital dimensions. An incalculable number. And yet Terran societies were so young, so fragile. It had taken them a short two hundred thousand years to go from cowering in caves to living in outer space. And for the last ten thousand years or so, since the rise of 'civilization,' Terra had been bound by wars, greed, and violence. Terrans suppressed others, enslaving them, crushing millions, and then billions under the boots of so few.

Aanji let those thoughts slide away as he pushed through each data wall, one after the other, in search of the woman he was supposed to meet.

Supposed to become.

Aanji found her consciousness in a North Dakota data wall, near a recreation of the original Turtle Mountain Indian Reservation, and loaded his Virtualis avatar near the field where she sat with some friends. Her name was Aanji Iron Woman. His namesake, though she didn't know it.

He inhaled the air and stared at the sunset clouds in the wide sky above him, the landscape easing itself into early summer. Powwow drums pounded in the distance. He marvelled at the perfect reality of it, from the slight chill of the soil to the prick of foxtail and bromegrass beneath his bare feet. He inhaled the scent, and sighed.

The woman looked over at him, her friends fading away as the data wall's memory program switched from nostalgia mode to real-time.

"It almost feels real enough to convince me," she said.

Aanji nodded. "They're getting better at simulation every year." He smiled and toed the dirt a minute, looking at the sky. "Have you thought more about what we discussed?" he asked.

She grinned at him. The lines of her faded brown skin hinted at the disease deep within her bones. "Yes, but isn't it dangerous for you?" she asked.

Aanji smiled. "All great things have greater risks. Sometimes the risk is part of the reason why you should do them." He held out a hand to her. She took it, and Aanji marvelled at the softness of her warm tiny fingers.

"It's the bannock," the woman said as she got up, grunting.

"I'm sorry?" Aanji asked.

"Bannock bread. When I make it here, using my nookomis' recipe, it tastes wrong. Not bad, but not the way I made it. You know. Before," the woman said gripping his hand. "Will it hurt?"

Aanji smiled. "Not at all." What he didn't say was that he'd found her physical body months ago, and had started doing the DNA extractions almost immediately. Illegal, of course, but at this point the risk was worth it.

The woman smiled, and together they walked on, over the hill.

Later, Aanji slipped back through the data wall's gel and carefully erased his tracks. Other Noncits who could trace him were too busy handling the usual flood of virtualized harassment against Citizens to even bother looking. Aanji stayed in the data world long enough to record the woman's peaceful death, and reroute the notification of her passing away from the morgue servers who would have sent a trundle cart for her body to undergo Renewal.

A moment later, he raced through the walls, rising up from the dream world of Virtualis back to his body. The chair he sat in chirped in alarm as he demanded the thing release him. For a moment the machine objected, but Aanji forced himself against the will of the simple safety protocol program and it relented in a series of error codes. The nanomaterials in his skin pulled back—he wondered if this was what getting stung by a bee swarm might feel like—and then the chair shoved him to his feet. He swayed a moment, the dim reality blurring his senses after the brightness of Virtualis.

Then he left in the direction of the station core, bare feet slapping against the concrete. In the transit corridors he hailed a bulbous station cart that was beetling by and hopped in. The door oozed back into place as he sat.

"Station identification and gene-classification, please," the trundle robot said politely in the rudest tone it could manage.

"Hey, you, stop! Hey, rat! Yeah, that's right. I'm talking to you. Don't walk away. You know who I am?"

Of course she knew. He was one of the Others. When he cornered her against the tan brick wall, he smelled like puke and beer and anger. Her eyes shot to the sidewalk. She said nothing. Talking would make it worse.

He grabbed her arm. Shook her until her carefully-composed neutrality crumbled. She trembled like a plastic bag in a tree during a storm.

"Answer me, dammit!"

"You're the police," she whispered. He made her say it again, louder. People hurried past them, eyes averted. She was alone.

"That's right. You have any money?"

She reached into her purse, her chest feeling like it was kindling into snapping flames of anger and shame.

Aanji sighed and held out his arm, rubbing the chair's nanomaterial with the outermost layer of the Chameleon Bag skin until the chrome gleamed.

"Vermis Limax, Seven Nine AIT Eight," he said, in as flat a tone as he could manage. The trundle bot extended a wand out that came over and wrapped around his arm like a slick tentacle. He forced himself not to shudder.

The wand whipped back and the trundle bot whined in alarm. Nanomaterial crawled over Aanji in thick ropey arms of hot gel, hardening into restraints that pinned him to the seat.

"This vehicle is not for noncitizen usage! Standby for arrest!"

Aanji frowned at this unexpected problem, but he was committed. He couldn't stop now. *She* needed him. He couldn't just abandon *her*.

"No."

He growled under his breath, brought his palm to his mouth and bit into the Chameleon skin. It screeched and crinkled, but Aanji yanked his arm away from his mouth, jaw clenched. The chrome flesh tasted like a burnt spoon. He shook himself and pressed the bare brown palm of the hand against the dash panel. Aanji spoke in a different pitch and timbre.

"Override the arrest command."

"Of course, Madam," the trundle bot purred. The restraint sizzled away, receding like sugar in salt water. "Where may I have the honour of taking you today?"

"Medical ward in Aquarius Nine, as quickly as possible," Aanji said, smug, and angry that *she* was treated so much better than Noncitizen Limax had been.

"Of course!" the trundle bot said cheerfully as it leaped into traffic on whirring insectile legs. Aanji frowned, inhaled, and started peeling off the rest the Chameleon skin, letting the chrome pieces fall to the floor in tatters. She tried to ignore the goosebumps rising on her naked body.

The trundle bot drummed through the Station, and Aanji started to believe that everything might work out after all. She leaned back into the plush seat and closed her eyes.

"We got lucky," she whispered. "If they don't chase you after the first mile they don't chase you." She laughed, easy and sonorous. She was no Korben Dallas, but this just might—

"TRANSIT UNIT19A! HALT!" boomed a voice that drowned out the traffic in the corridor. The trundle cart hiccuped to a sudden stop.

"Maybe it's two miles," Aanji said, cursing.

A black, ten-meter-high security pod rolled up,lights flashing. Traffic in the transit lane flowed around it like a river of metallic ants. Three guards sprang from the security pod and pointed stun rods at the trundle cart.

"Vermis Limax, Seven Nine, step out of the transit unit!"

Aanji clenched her teeth and reached for the door panel.

The trundle cart swivelled a speaker panel towards the guards. "Please move," it said, with the tone of a very patient if put-upon machine. "There is no one by that name in this transit unit, and we are in a hurry."

The lead security guard tilted its mirrored head, frowning.

"You have a fugitive Noncit aboard. Open the doors immediately."

The trundle cart shivered a moment, in what Aanji could only interpret as a sigh. The trundle cart rolled forward, the speaker panel oozing up until it was level with the guard's face.

"You know, Security Unit HA3, you're violating my client's civil liberties here. If you attempt to *kidnap* my fare, who has the mitochondrial profile of a full Citizen, I will be forced to defend them, and report you to the Citizens Right Board!"

"Are you daft?" HA3 said, sputtering. "You are clearly carrying a fugitive of the law! Check their genetic profile agai—"

The trundle cart jerked sideways into the transit lanes with indignation, legs whirring as it scampered towards the hospital. "The absolute NERVE of that security unit! Can you believe that? Talk about rude!"

There was a loud siren screech, and suddenly all vehicles in the transit corridor slowed to a halt.

Aanji's stomach clenched. Looking backwards she saw the the security pod spider-leaping through traffic toward them. She ducked lower in the seat.

"Are you pulling my crashbars? I am *so* filing a civil rights complaint!" The trundle cart cursed in some strange Assembly language and leaped, jumping over cars and transit bundles.

"Transit Unit 191A, stop! You are in direct contradiction of order—"

"Oh, put a prop shaft in it and spin off with your power hungry orders! I have a Citizen on board!" yelled 191A as it leaped down an adjoining corridor, bouncing down pedestrian walkways like a headless bunny. There was a loud pop and sizzle as a stun bolt hit the back of the trundle cart.

"Assault! This is a crime!" screeched the cart as it ejected two rear legs that had been struck, shifted, and started galloping like a horse. Aanji was trying hard not to be sick. The trundle cart must have noticed.

"Go ahead!" it said, "Throw up, I could use the extra nanomass! I'll even take it off your fare."

"I'll pass, if that's all righ—" Another crackling pop, this one more feeling than noise. Aanji was thrown to the side of the cart as the tunnel spun in her vision, lights and cars flying overhead as they rolled. There was a screeching bang and suddenly her shoulder hurt. Then everything stopped and the cart spasmed a moment.

"This is bad," groaned the trundle cart. "I had no idea those tyrants would turn terrorist to get you. I can take you to the end of the hallway just down there, but you'll have to run after that."

Aanji cursed herself, wiping her eyes with the back of her palms. "No, I'll get out here. You need to stay safe. How much do I owe you?"

"Just go!" 191A said as the panel nearest the corridor to safety oozed away to allow Aanji out.

"Thank you!" she said, but the scorched trundle cart scrambled back and leaped the way they came before she could finish. There was a ground-shaking explosion. Aanji felt the lurch of weightlessness and the station lighting switched over from white to red, then dark blue as the power in their section dimmed.

She started striding towards the Aquarius Nine hospital. Blue lights and deep black shadows spilled through the corridors.

After a minute, the lights switched back to red, and the familiar pull of the station's engines creating spin gave Aanji's body a gentle tug. There was another echoing boom behind her, and the metronome clink-clack of footsteps following. She broke into a dead sprint. She made it near the retail area just a kilometre away from the hospital when she felt something cold and wet smack her in the back. There was a flare of pain that stole her breath before she could scream, and she was thrown forward. Aanji hit the deck and rolled.

She was riding her mountain bike through the woods just south of her village when the rock hit her in the back of the neck. Bubbles of pain washed through her head then, hissing like grains of sand in an underwater tide.

"Get back here, you bitch!" a man screamed as she climbed back on her bike, desperate to escape. A pale hand flew into her face and then she was yanked away.

"Why you running, plugger?" asked the guard as she lay flat on her back. The guard grinned, coldly. "You think your injections and implants can fool us? We know what you are, you deceptive little witch. You can do all the pills and surgeries you want, you'll always be the same trashy Noncit."

Aanji's awareness blossomed with greasy fire as the guard kicked her in the stomach. She slid across the deck plating so fast, the glass wall that stopped her cracked into spiderwebs before exploding, raining crystalline flakes down on her. She coughed and tried to scramble to her feet. The guard was on her instantly, hammering her with fists as hard as steel and she fell hard on her face, cutting her lip.

She brought her hands over her head, her elbows blocking her face as she curled into the fetal position and coughed blood. At some point, the sound went all cotton, and she receded from the pain.

Days earlier he was kissing her behind the high school, and for once, she'd let him. She'd let go as his hands wandered her hips, his stubbled chin causing her to shiver as he kissed her neck. She'd been so scared, then, of his rough hands, and so excited at the same time.

Now he and his cousins stood over her, chunks of concrete in their fists. She was already bleeding and bruised, the rock to the back of her neck left her dizzy. She wondered if she was going to die.

What for? For the sin of letting one of the Others kiss her? For kissing back? For enjoying it? The man who put his lips on hers now raised the rock, and she raised broken arms, whimpering.

And then—

There was a screech, and a scream of lightning striking metal. Aanji was only dimly aware of it. Someone had stopped the guard from killing her. There was yelling, but it all sounded underwater.

A familiar voice. "Of course she's human, you idiot! Look at the blood on her!"

"Perie, it's a trick!" That was the guard's voice. *Perie?* The guard continued, "She's using skinplants to create a false genetic profile! She's not human, she's just trying to trick everyone! Look at her mods! She's a warped plugger!"

"Even if she *was* a plugger, you have no right to beat her to death!"

"She's a noncitizen! She'll live! And this will stop her from running next time!"

There was a loud clang in the hazy darkness of Aanji's pain, followed by a gasp.

"Perie!" yelled the guard, sounding winded. Aanji opened her eyes, and saw a blurred figure sitting on the deck. The world lurched out of focus. She tried to sit up, and the world slid down to black.

She must not have been unconscious long. When she woke up she was clothed in a grey jumpsuit, and leaning against the glass pillar opposite the one that she'd broken earlier. Perie was holding her upright, a frown in her masculine face.

"Are you sure you won't come for dinner and a movie?" Perie whispered.

Aanji laughed, and started coughing. "You know I don't do romance," she said when she could speak. "I don't have those urges. No offense."

Perie nodded her head, the hulking muscles framing a sweet, square face and gentle eyes. "I had to try one last time. Listen, I've got to get Ghengimax here back to the scene of the accident and make the transit unit's mess go away. So I can't help you past here. But, that doesn't mean I don't care. Send me a message when you get there, alright?"

Aanji nodded, and hugged the woman, her facial hair tickling Aanji's face. Then Perie was gone. Aanji stayed there a moment, waiting until her nausea dulled from a raging storm, before walking the rest of the way to Aquarius Nine's hospital.

"Just sit down in this chair, miss, and we'll see to your wounds. What's your name?" asked a nurse who rushed to her when she entered the lobby.

"What? No, I'm—I'm fine, I don't need treatment," Aanji started to say. But the nurse called for a medical chair and a doctor.

"Nonsense! You've got blood and bruises all over you," chided the nurse gently as they guided her over to the medchair.

"No, that's not bloo—" Aanji started. Then she held her hands up to see for herself. Her hands were streaked with bright *red* blood. She started crying.

"Are you sure you're okay to refuse treatment?" asked the nurse who walked with Aanji to the restroom.

She nodded, and sniffled. "I just…need to get cleaned up before I see my friend." The nurse nodded.

Aanji went to the sinks and stared at her face. She could see the injection sites' ghosted scars, but apparently no one else did. But it was the blood that shocked her the most. It was bright red. She didn't want to clean it off. She was in agonizing pain, but the sight of her own blood gave her butterflies in her stomach that filled her with a warm joy she'd never truly felt before. Still, she spent ten minutes washing up. She inhaled a deep breath and stepped outside, trying to think of an excuse for the nurse. But the woman was gone.

Aanji turned to the elevators and went to the floor of the woman she "killed" in Virtualis. The woman was still alive, but brain dead. Only Aanji's programming, nestled in the data world, kept the hospital's automated life support systems on, thinking she was still in a dream state.

Aanji held the woman's hand. After a few minutes, she pulled the IV from the bag, and set up a transfusion line leading from the woman into her own vein. It wasn't as clean as getting a pure DNA replication from the injector gun, but she could collect enough blood to synthesize a replica profile.

She hoped.

After Aanji left the hospital, she dialled up her old work access system, and erased herself from its files. At the same time, the dead woman's body was being processed for burial on Terra. Aanji kept her word.

She stood in line at the departures area for boarding the Seed ships.

"Excuse me, Citizen. Will you present your identification and gene-classification, please?" asked the boarding attending with a smile.

"You wanna see my ID?" the woman in the uniform yelled. She stepped back from the girl. "This is my badge, and that's my squad car, and this is my god damned gun!" The police officer, one of the Others, pulled the pistol out and pointed it at the girl's face. Except now it was Aanji's face. She grinned.

"Of course," Aanji said. As she held her arm out, she knew. The sudden visions weren't daydreams or hallucinations, but the other Aanji's memories.

The attendant waved a sensor-wand over her arm with a smile. For a second, Aanji wondered if she'd be caught, arrested and executed for trying to board the Seed Ship bound for Gliese 667 Cc. But the wand stayed silent.

After a minute, Aanji was walking down the long concourse towards the generation ship, a kilometres-long asteroid with coiled rings trailing behind it, and city-sized engines at the back.

A few of the people on the Seed ship knew that wasn't really Aanji Iron Woman in the jingle dress, dancing with the others around the bonfire. They also knew there was earth from old Terra in the soil here, but it was not the Turtle Island of old. They were Heaven Walkers now, and they adapted, to preserve the old ways. The buffalo that grazed in the distance did not care, and the stars overhead still sang to them. And they were given a chance to thrive. So, even if Aanji Iron Woman was not the daughter they remembered, she kept to the old ways, and that was good enough.

As for Aanji Iron Woman, as she danced in the night, carefully following the steps of her aunties, nothing else but this moment mattered. She might never pass as human the way she wanted to, but to the Star River tribe, she was family.

•●•●•●•

VALEDICTION AT THE STAR VIEW MOTEL

by Nathan Adler

"WHAT DID YOU SAY ABOUT MY SISTER?"

"Your sist—?" Was all Charlene managed to say before Eadie's fist connected with the girl's eye. Charlene's head snapped back with the force of the blow, and she reeled and doubled over, palm cupped to the site of the injury. Charlene wouldn't make that mistake again.

Charlene hadn't even spilled her drink, though—Eadie would give her that—left hand held above her head to keep the brown beer bottle level, just-suppressed sobs hidden beneath her heavy breathing.

Eadie was one of the 'white-kids.' White-as-white-could-be with her pale blonde hair lighter than strawberry, now neon-pink to match the stud in her lip. But she'd also been adopted by the Neyananoosics. More than one white kid realized their mistake when she drew attention to their racist bullshit.

Case in point: Charlene.

A few minutes earlier, Charlene had started in. "Look at that chick over there," she'd indicated with a lift of her chin. "I bet she's screwed half the town by now." Sitting on a log on the other side of the fire was Eadie's younger step-sister Cadence, and some punk who was clearly keen on her. Charlene obviously hadn't realized Cadence and Eadie were sisters.

There was some hooting and hollering from the guys around the fire at the potential cat-fight, but the confrontation was over quickly, with Charlene now holding her beer bottle to her eye to keep the swelling down, her boyfriend Jordie comforting her as she whined: "How was I supposed to know they were sisters!?"

"I told you to watch what you say around here. This isn't Sterling..." Eadie heard Jordie say as he led his girlfriend to the opposite side of the bonfire, at the edge of the ring of light; as. far away as they could get from Eadie without actually leaving the flickering, popping radius cast by the flames.

"Eadie talks with her fists."

After the brief outburst of violence, the laughter and chatter of the party resumed, rising and falling in waves from the various groups congregated around the fire.

This sort of misunderstanding happened more often since she'd returned home the year before last. At sixteen, Eadie left foster care and came back to Ghost Lake. By then, many people had forgotten her. But the Neyananoosics never forgot. They raised Eadie before her biological mother died, before Children's Aide swooped in to take her. The whole system was wrong, preferring that she live with messed-up people of her own race instead of a caring family who loved her.

Eadie hadn't really felt like going to the bonfire, even though it was a Friday night, but she knew Cadence planned on being there. She wanted to keep an eye on her. So Eadie went too. Separately, though, to give Cadence's space. On the way to the party, Eadie stopped at the Star View Motel, looking up at the unlit sign, the logo of a tree-line silhouette backlit by the night sky. It had once belonged to her Uncle Oogie, before his life spiralled out of control. Before he hit the alcohol and drugs pretty hard, before he ended up in jail. Eadie had been too young to know what sent him off the rails. She thought he was still alive somewhere. Maybe. Maybe not. Maybe he was dead. There was an ache in her chest, squeezing, the way she imagined a mild heart attack would feel.

They weren't blood-related, but Eadie remembered one time when Oogie took her and her siblings out for ice cream at the Cream Queen on

Violin Road in Sterling. She remembered his gap-toothed smile, too. He was always smiling, even though it made him look like a pumpkin.

Eadie and her siblings had stayed up all night to watch the Leonid meteor shower.

"It only happens once every thirty-three years, you know?"

The telescope was set up at the edge of the parking lot. They roasted marshmallows, the glow of their campfire—the only source of light pollution—contained within the rusted metal O-ring of a tire. In the background was the static and pop of the baby monitor in case Eadie's sisters woke up in the night. Kylie and Cadence, being younger, had already been put to bed, so it was just Eadie and her brothers, Peyton, Sion, and Severn. Bundled up in their winter clothes, earmuffs, and scarves, with mugs of steaming hot chocolate from a thermos, and the rhythm of Oogie's voice as he told stories about the constellations. The Wintermaker and the Underwater Panther. The Sweat-Lodge. Moose, Crane, Loon, and Fisher. The Road of All Souls, and Hole in the Day.

"A *meteoroid* is part of an asteroid or comet. It's called a *meteor* if it burns up as it enters the Earth's atmosphere, and a *meteorite* if it actually hits the ground."

An observatory had been built north of Ghost Lake, probably owing to the uncommon lack of light pollution and the clarity of the night skies. Maybe that was what triggered Oogie's love of astronomy?

One by one, Eadie's brothers slowly dropped off to sleep as exhaustion overcame excitement. Eadie's eyelids felt heavy, too, though she struggled to stay awake, to see every last streak of light as it sped across the sky.

"Do you see that?" Oogie's voice hushed. Eadie's eyelids opened in time to see a meteor blaze across the sky, so bright it blocked out the light of the other stars, creating its own halo of day, so close it seemed to hit the ground just over the next rise. She knew it must've been an optical illusion because she would have felt the thud of impact if it hit the ground.

"A meteorite!"

Eadie turned to her brothers, but they were fast asleep in their fold-up chairs.

"Anang." Uncle Oogie smiled his pumpkin-faced smile, his eyes sparkling and his cheeks ruddy with the cold. Eadie shared the smile; co-conspirators. The only ones to have witnessed the magic moment. Anang. *Star.*

She'd fallen asleep not long after, the brightest of meteors illuminating her dreams.

She'd felt a distant lightness as Oogie carried her to bed. She knew that he must have carried each of her siblings, one by one, to their beds, too. They'd been up way past their bedtimes.

But that was many years ago.

Eadie stood in Oogie's old Star View Motel, looking up at a hole in the roof where the rain had got in. Ironic, now, that stars were actually visible from inside. Though the windows were boarded up, teenagers had pried apart the soft plywood and squeezed in through the smashed glass. Stepping through the window frame, she felt the glass grinding beneath her combat boots. The occasional party or hook-up took place here. The occasional transient would sleep in an old motel bed. Most of the rooms were undamaged, though the building as a whole was in bad shape—especially here, where a sapling grew in the middle of the room, bathed in a beam of moonlight. Nature was slowly reclaiming its rightful place. Water stains and algae mould crawled up the peeling walls.

Had that shooting star really been a meteorite? Or had it burned up in the atmosphere, before it ever had the chance to hit the ground? Every time she went for a hike, Eadie wondered about it. If one day she might find it.

The party was in the forest, a short walk from the motel, out past the old Anishinaabeg version of a Totem pole surrounded by disintegrating railing and rusty nails. Far enough away from the road that the noise and light wouldn't attract attention. There wasn't all that much to do in Ghost Lake or the nearby town of Cheapaye. The name was a perversion of an Ojibwa word—*Jiibay,* the same name as the lake.

Jiibay meant *ghost.*

Eadie had never seen one. But there were lots of stories.

The motel wasn't haunted as far as Eadie knew, though it stirred up memories. A dusty sadness sifted down in the still air, her thoughts as sad as the old Star View itself. She picked her way through the rubble of broken beer bottles, human excrement, and smashed furniture, and finally made her way to the fresh air outside. She stepped away from the crumbling motel and towards the party.

It was that ugly tail-end of winter, when all the snow was mostly melted, revealing all the hidden garbage underneath, but it was still cold enough that Eadie's breath was visible with every exhale. When she got to the bonfire, she hung back, watching the revelry. Kids from Ghost Lake and kids from Cheapaye. Mostly Indians. But some white kids, too. Clumps of teenagers sitting on felled log benches. The fire pit had been dug deep, and you couldn't stand too close for the heat.

There was Garion, wearing black and steadily feeding the fire, dragging entire branches out of the bush. The fire danced in the twin pupil of his eyes, like mirrors reflecting his soul. A natural born fire-starter. Eadie wondered if he'd ever received fire-keeper teachings. The bonfire was too large to jump across, though that didn't stop kids from trying and getting their asses burnt.

It was a stupid game. Entertaining, but stupid.

That's when Charlene had sidled up to her, probably thinking Eadie was another white girl she could bond with over white girl things and oh-so-casual us-versus-them racism, despite the fact that that Charlene's boyfriend Jordie was an Indian.

Mushkeg was at that field party, too, in a leather fringe jacket with a matching fringe purse, bright red lipstick, and highheels. Native high-fashionista. Rez-chic. Man, was Mushkeg ever beautiful. Forties harido like a World War II nurse, tresses piled up on top of her head in waves. Eadie noticed Mushkeg smiling at her from across the flames, watching through a bird-cage veil as the scuffle with Charlene played out. Was it approval at how Eadie handled herself? Derisiveness? Amusement?

Eadie learned in art class that the eye went to the point of highest contrast. Maybe that's what Mushkeg was, and why Eadie's eyes went to her. A point of high contrast.

Eadie's own fashion sense tended more towards grunge/punk-rock than high-fashion-anything. It was a lot easier to dump a new shade of Kool-Aid in her hair each week than to attempt an elaborate style.

"Hey chick-itaaa kwe!" Mushkeg made her way over, flask held high, hips swaying in a way Eadie could only think of as a runway model *sashay*. How could she walk in those heels? "I like your style."

Eadie didn't get the sense that Mush was referring to her outfit Faded jean jacket sloppily stitched with patches from various bandripped green cargo pants, and boots she'd gotten from an army surplus store.

"Thanks." Eadie said, feeling her cheeks flush.

"You're plucky, just like Tinker Bell." Mush took a sip from the metal flask, her face puckered. "Good shit."

Eadie waggled her fingers. "I will curdle your milk and make your livestock sick." Mushkeg giggled, much to Eadie's relief. It was a lame joke. Humour could fall flat and make things awkward.

"Tink isn't a *witch*," Mushkeg said, one eye scrunched up. "She's a *fairy*."

Eadie snorted. "What does that make you? Peter Pan?"

"Tiger Lily, of course. Fuck Peter Pan." Mushkeg flicked her head, as if to use the motion to toss hair out of her eyes. But her hair was pinned up now, so it stayed immobile. The interlaced web of the fishnet-veil made her look glamorous, like some sort of film noir star.

"I always wanted to be one of the lost boys." Mushkeg raised her eyes to the sky, maybe searching for that second-star-to-the-right, past the glare of the bonfire and the brightness of the moon. "I never wanted to grow up."

"Who does?" Eadie took one last puff on her cigarette, and then crushed it out on the log they were sitting on. She needed to quit. Maybe next week.

Mushkeg held her flask out, eyebrow raised. Eadie took a swig—it was Rusty. Eadie hadn't figured the girl for a whiskey drinker. It had a slight sweetness that burned on the way down.

Mushkeg nodded. "Wish fulfillment, I guess."

Eadie often had the same thought. Press the right buttons, light up those pleasure centres of the brain, and you'd get the correct results. Carve he brain into components and people weren't all that complicated. Eadie had her fair share of social workers trying to analyze her, to explain why she "acted out." That psycho-babble was easy to pick up.

"The unconscious repression of desire?"

"Repressed? Who said I'm repressed?" Mushkeg's voice pitched high. "Fuck Freud. *And* his damned cigar." She took a haul on her cigarette, red lips melodramatically pursed around the filter.

"I always thought Peter Pan was gay."

"Because of the tights?" Mushkeg had a shrill laugh, and Eadie couldn't tell at first if it was real or if she was just pretending. She decided no one would pretend to have such an ugly laugh.

Eadie launched into it. "What was so horrible about Victorian England, that Pan had to retreat into a fantasy world of make-believe? One where he would never have to grow up, or face his latent homosexuality."

"That's so twisted!" Mushkeg cackled. Eadie felt a warm glow spread through her ribs that had nothing to do with the Rusty, pleased that her rant was being met with amusement.

It emboldened her to keep going, leaning in and dropping her voice to a deeper, wispier register. "Wendy, Tiger Lily, Tink—even the bloody mermaids—they all want him *baaad*. But Pan? He only has eyes for his lost boys."

"Well *I'm* not repressed!" Mushkeg sat with her back straight, shoulders pushed back in defiance, eyes flashing about the clearing. The heat crept up Eadie's neck and into her cheeks. She was up in the clouds, tingling. Eadie didn't want to get her hopes up if she was misreading the signs. But, screw it! No pain, no gain. If she didn't take risks and play the game, there'd be no way she'd ever have a chance of winning. Right?

Or losing. But she quickly pushed that thought aside.

She eyed her sister Cadence, laughing amongst her circle of friends, the rangy boy still fawning over her. She trusted Cadence enough not to get knocked up, anyway.

"Come on." Eadie took Mushkeg's hand, and pulled her to her feet. But the flask had been raised mid-drink, so Mushkeg spluttered and choked, laughing.

"Hey! That's good shit. Yer making me waste it!"

Eadie could feel Charlene tracking them as they left the circle of light cast by the bonfire, still enfolded in the shelter of Jordie's arms. Eadie certainly didn't care what that townie thought. She was probably going to spread nasty lies about her. Eadie knew the type, and was happy she'd hit her as hard as she had. The fight was over before it started, but Eadie would still have to deal with the fallout later.

They paused on the wooden footbridge spanning Tyner's Creek.

"Some kid died here. You know?"

"I know." Eadie nodded. Everyone had heard the story. An urban legend, really. It was said the spirit of a small child walked the shore's edge, haunting the river where he'd been murdered. 'Tyner' was an Anglicization of the original 'Tynuck.' Whether the story was real or not, the origins of the name was likely pre-colonial.

This close to the source of the spring, the water was pure and clean, unadulterated by the dilution of runoff and the various tributaries that would sully it before it joined with the larger body of Ghost Lake. The source for the stream was actually subterranean, so it was a popular place for people to come and collect fresh spring water.

Mushkeg and Eadie peered over the railing, watching the water rush by below, bubbles and froth floating on the surface of the churning river.

"Hcccuuaaacchk, chhhkkkkaaaccht."

Mushkeg stood on tip-toes, her high-heels perched on the railing as she horked a loogie over the side. They watched as the ball of spittle, phlegm, and snot separated, and spun about by its center of mass, connected by a thin, translucent strand before landing on the surface of the water, just another bit of froth carried away on the swiftly moving surface. It was mesmerizing.

"That was very attractive."

"I do try," Mushkeg smiled.

They made their way through the trees and across the barren parking lot of the Star View, walking across chewed up asphalt and the lines of faded yellow paint to one of the motel's rooms.

"How do you have a key?" Mushkeg raised an eyebrow as Eadie flipped through her keyring. She fit the correct one into the lock, and felt the vibration as the deadbolt *shuffed* aside.

"My uncle Oogie gave it to me. A long time ago. Back when he was still running the motel—just in case I ever needed a place to stay."

"Oh, right. I keep forgetting you're a 'Noosic."

"You and everybody else," Eadie muttered as the door swung open and the stale air trapped inside wafted out. It was musty, but the roof hadn't caved in here so there was no mould or mildew, just the drab brown carpets, grey coverlet, peach walls, and green drapes. Eadie tried the light switch, but of course it didn't work. The power had been shut off long ago, so she opened the curtains to let in natural light from the moon, metal loops sliding across the metal rung with a *shfff*. At least it was relatively warm away from the windchill.

"Is your dad ever going to do anything with this old place?

"I think he's still hoping Oogie will come back one day."

"Sad."

"This is the honeymoon suite." Eadie swiped her arms to the left and right to clear a path through the cobwebs. "It's the only room with a chimney."

"You know you're never further than three feet away from a spider."

"Uounhh," Eadie shuddered. "That's not true!"

"Well. In most natural environments. They occupy almost every ecological niche. Want to know how many pounds of bugs people eat in their lifetime, just from the ones that fall into our food?"

"Okay," Eadie held up her hand. "Let me stop you there."

"—estimated, like, one or two pounds! Per year!"

Mushkeg knelt before the interlocking stone of the hearth, holding a butane lighter to some crumpled napkins that still had the ruby impression of her lips. Within moments, the old dry logs in the fireplace were lit, and the flames threw a cheerful glow that quickly spread to the rest of the room.

"How'd you do that?" Eadie asked.

"Do what?" Mushkeg rolled back on her heels. The stiletto-spiked boots were the kind Elvira would wear. Mushkeg certainly had the boobs for it. Elvira boobs.

"Get the fire going so fast. Like some sort of wizard."

"Magic." Mushkeg said, her face scrunching up in a smile.

"I don't believe in magic." The stillness of the motel infected Eadie again with its melancholy silence.

"Everybody's got some kind of magic." Mushkeg plunked down on the mattress, her boobs bouncing with the bed-springs. "Even if they don't know it."

"Wait, what's your magic?"

"I thought you said you didn't believe in magic?" Mush smiled, eyes sparkling, a hint of purple eye-shadow amongst the coal. *I'm not going to tell you unless you tell me you believe.* "Every time you say that, a fairy dies."

"Oh, come on!" Eadie rolled her eyes and flopped onto the bed. "Tell me."

"Have you ever read *Charlotte's Web*?"

Eadie frowned. "Yeah. And I saw movie—the cartoon."

"Well, that's my magic. That's what I can do."

"You can talk to spiders!?" Eadie's lip curled, the backing on the pink stud scraping against her teeth. When she was nervous, she couldn't keep her tongue from feeling around the crevices of the piercing. A nervous tic.

"Nooo! Well—not exactly." She looked down at the patterned carpeting on the floor. Shrugged. "They talk to me. Same thing."

Eadie propped herself up on one elbow. "Can you get them to write letters in a spider web?"

"I don't know," Mushkeg tilted her head. "I've never tried."

"So you're more like Templeton."

"Templeton was the rat!"

"It's either that or the pig."

"Fern! I'm the girl! Fern! Obviously."

"Goof!" Eadie hit Mush with a motel pillow. Mush squealed, picked up a pillow.

"Errr, not so hard, you dweeb!"

"Hoser."

"Khcnunh khcnunh khcnunh." Eadie made oinking sounds. "Templeton! Wilbur!"

"I yield! I yield!"

Eadie held the pillow above her head, poised for another blow. Mush's hair was disarranged, make-up smudged, eyes squinted shut. Eadie dropped the pillow, performing a reverse push up to bring her face close to Mushkeg's. And kissed her. Mushkeg's eyes flew open in surprise for a moment before her lips melted into the kiss, and her eyelids flickered shut again.

Eadie pulled back after a minute like a swimmer surfacing for air.

Mush's dark eyes filled her vision, reflecting the light from the moon—it was close to being full, though it was hard to tell, sometimes.

Feathers from the down-filled pillows drifted around them like they were inside a giant, shaken snow-globe. A fox in a henhouse. Chicken slaughterhouse. Pillow factory that had exploded. Silver-blue spotlight of the moon.

"It's a full moon." Mush said.

"How can you tell?"

"We're in sync, me and her. Like werewolves."

Eadie raised her head and howled, and Mushkeg joined her. They were werewolves now, they were changing, metamorphosing, their clothes ripped as their limbs elongated, shredded in the sudden urgency to get at the meat of each other's bodies, as if they really were wolves, instead of just pretending.

Mush lay back, naked on the floral-patterned bedspread, her hands reaching toward Eadie, drawing her down. The air was cool on their bare flesh, but Eadie didn't care. They'd make their own heat. Eadie leaned down into the kiss, and in a flash Mushkeg had raised herself up on her side and flipped Edie over, so Eadie was now looking up into Mush's eyes. Sparkling. Her hair had escaped the elaborate system of loops and whorls which had kept it imprisoned. Now it fell down in waves. Framing her face. A dark Botticelli.

Then Mush's lips were on hers again. And the room slowly grew warmer with their heat, and from the heat of the flames in the hearth.

"So what's my magic, then?" Eadie asked.

"I don't know." Mushkeg's eyes slid around the room, finding the darker shadows. "You probably just haven't found it yet. Some people never do. Blame it on bad luck, the weather, some external factor, never recognizing it." Her red lips puckered. Like a pixie. If Eadie was Tink—which pixie was Mush?

"Spiders creep me out."

"No! They're artists! They weave the most beautiful patterns. And they keep your dreams safe—where do you think us Ojibeways got the idea for the dream-catcher?"

"Did the spiders tell you that?" Eadie tickled the other girl's ribs with a stray pinion feather. Mush armed herself, and things quickly devolved into a squirming, laughter-and-scream-filled tickle fight. Eadie wondered why she was she being so silly. Eadie was a punk-rocker. She kicked butt. She didn't giggle. But something about Mush made her feel like being silly.

They fell asleep, tangled in the sheets and in each other's arms, the heat of the fire slowly dwindling, with only the heat of their own bodies keeping each other warm.

When Eadie woke up, the room was cold, the fire had burned down to ash, and Mushkeg had gone. Bright sunlight illuminated the windows with a warm yellow glow, misty where it refracted through the gauzy material of the curtain.

What did it mean that Mush had left without saying anything, while Eadie was still asleep? Without waking her up, or saying goodbye, or letting her know that she was leaving? Was Mushkeg upset? Was she feeling guilty or ashamed? Did she regret hooking up with another chick?

Eadie stretched and yawned, looking around for her shirt. There was no use panicking. Mushkeg could have left for any number of reasons. To get home before dark so her parents wouldn't discover that she'd been out all night. To avoid awkward morning conversations. Maybe she had somewhere to be early, and she needed to get ready. Maybe she just didn't want to wake Eadie up. She had been sleeping so peacefully.

In the dim bathroom, Eadie turned on the taps to scrub her face, but of course the water didn't work. It had been shut off where the pipes entered the building to keep the pipes from freezing and exploding during the winter. Damn.

Eadie looked up at her face in the mirror, then let her features blur as she shifted focus to what had been drawn in blood-red lipstick—the colour of fire engines and flames—inside a heart.

xoxoxoxo, the ten digits of a cell phone number, signed 'Mushk' with a long trailing "k." For a moment they were together in the mirror, Mushkeg and Eadie floating inside the thick red outline of a heart.

Eadie smiled, losing some of the tension in her shoulders now that she knew Mushkeg hadn't simply ditched her like the Queen song, loving and leaving her. Feeling floaty, she drifted out to tidy the room.

To make it look as if no one had been there.

Eadie went to draw the curtains, to close the Star View parking lot from the window. That's when she saw the delicate tracery of lines, only visible because of the intensity of the morning sunlight, so finely woven, the strands would have gone unnoticed in any other kind of light. A web of lines, radiating outward like the central arms of a spiral galaxy. So thin, the silk danced in the slight exhalation of her breath.

A spider's web.

And amongst the delicate tracery of lines, a word written in spider's silk.

A word. Blurring, as her eyes filled with tears.

Anang. *Star.*

Mii'isa Minik.

The End

•●•●•●•

PARALLAX

by Cleo Keahna

Boy rested breasts tethered
to his alarm clock with electrical tape
Weighing in as if to say "Wake Up:
You're dreaming boyhood into life again
You're faking manhood into strife again

There's a fiddle on the mantelpiece
I ain't touched it since ten ago, at least
Was that mess-chord something trauma, or
Was it the midnight sonata that hurt most?
Yeah, it was Tuesday, and 3 in the p.m.,
    when all the grownups got no eyebrows
    & none of the eyebrows got grownups, but listen:
You calling yourself Boy at cheekbone
them's no reason to contradict you. Hear?

10 years old––
    if'n you step to the side,
    or wake the long way home,
    fiddle mantelpiece down the line you'll be a "self-made man."
But you took the short route, and barefoot! clumsy first moon,
bending your brows with brand-name pomade every *bzzt.*

So when you reach that ciggy drafting ballot age,
They'll still be calling you Miss, cor you missed
        ya shot, soldier, an' ye missed,
        there were a draft here, soldier,
you missed i'eh--
        You manmade self.
        If you quit taping at 18 they might sincerely crown you "Sir;"
        You just oughta know when to step aside.

Now here we Mmph. & of the ride.
You keep pomade, stop sonata,
it's a silent mindy, here inside.

No chance to Miss-Step if you know where to hide.
You chance a misstep when there's nowhere to hide.

•●•●•●•

BIOS

NATHAN ADLER is a writer and artist, who works in many different mediums, including audio, video, drawing & painting, as well as glass. His novel *Wrist* is published by Kegedonce Press (July 2016). He has a short story in *The Playground of Lost Toys* (Exile Dec. 2015), and a forthcoming story, "Tyner's Creek" in an anthology of, *Canadian Creatures, Monsters and Myth* (Exile 2016). He is a member of Lac Des Mille Lacs First Nation.

GWEN BENAWAY is of Anishinaabe and Métis descent. Her first collection of poetry, *Ceremonies for the Dead,* was published in 2013 and her second collection of poetry, *Passage,* is forthcoming from Kegedonce Press in Fall 2016. As emerging Two-Spirited poet, she has been described as the spiritual love child of Thompson Highway and Sylvia Plath. In 2015, she was the recipient of the inaugural Speaker's Award for a Young Author and in 2016 received an Dayne Ogilvie Honour of Distinction from the Writer›s Trust of Canada. Her work has been published and anthologized internationally. She and her many vintage dresses can be found on Instagram @gwenbenaway

DARCIE LITTLE BADGER is a Lipan Apache writer, comic creator, and phytoplankton geneticist. Much like the plankton she studies, DLB drifts around, as if untethered to the land. She shares her life with a pound puppy named Rosie. DLB's short fiction has appeared in places like *Strange Horizons* and *No Sh!t, There I Was: An Anthology of Improbable Tales.* Follow her on Twitter at @ShiningComic.

DANIEL HEATH JUSTICE (Cherokee Nation) is Canada Research Chair in Indigenous Literature and Expressive Culture and Professor of First Nations and Indigenous Studies and English at the University of British Columbia. A literary and cultural studies scholar as well as a fantasy writer, he has published and edited extensively in the field of Indigenous literary studies, including the recent *Oxford Handbook of Indigenous American Literature* (co-edited with James H. Cox). He is also the author of two volumes in the Animal Series from Reaktion Books (UK), including *Badger* and the forthcoming *Raccoon,* as well as the epic Indigenous fantasy novel, *The Way of Thorn and Thunder: The Kynship Chronicles.*

CLEO KEAHNA is an Ojibwe and Meskwaki artist. He has been published once before, in the Spring 2016 issue of the *Split Rock Review.* Many of his stories draw on personal experience and a desire to ruin the English language. He also plays the lead role in the independent drama film *Six and Bisti,* which is aiming for a 2017 release.

MARI KURISATO is the pen name for a disabled, LGBTQIA, tribally enrolled Cote First Nations Ojibwe woman who lives in Denver Colorado with her wife and son. She has written two self-published books, and her short fiction has appeared in MBRANE-SF, the *Things We Are Not* anthology, and is forthcoming to Northwest Press. She is currently hard at work on her next novel, seeking an agent, and spending too much time on Twitter & in MMO's. Find her on twitter at @CyborgN8VMari & polychromantium.com

DAVID ALEXANDER ROBERTSON, of Irish, Scottish, English, and Cree heritage, has created several bestselling graphic novels, including the *7 Generations* series, the *Tales From Big Spirit* series, as well as his newest graphic *novel Betty: The Helen Betty Osborne Story.* He was a contributor to the anthologies *Manitowapow: Aboriginal Writings From the Land of*

Water and *Moonshot: The Indigenous Comics Collection*. His first novel, *The Evolution of Alice*, was published in fall 2014, and he won the John Hirsch Award for Most Promising Manitoba Writer in 2015.

RICHARD VAN CAMP is an internationally renowned storyteller and best-selling author with 20 books out in the past 20 years. His novel, The Lesser Blessed, recently celebrated its 20th anniversary and is now a feature film with First Generation Films. His comics and graphic novels deal with sexual health (*Kiss Me Deadly*), gang prevention (*Path of the Warrior*), peace-making (Eisner-nominated *A Blanket of Butterflies*), restorative justice (*Three Feathers*) and mental health (*The Blue Raven.*) You can visit him on Facebook, Twitter or at richardvancamp.com